CANNIBAL KISS

CANNIBAL KISS

a novel by
DANIEL ODIER

translated by
LANIE GOODMAN

Random House New York

*Grateful acknowledgment is made to the following for permission to reprint
previously published material:*
CAROL MANN AGENCY: Excerpts from *Red Giants, White Dwarfs* by Robert
Jastrow. Copyright © 1979 by Reader's Library, Inc. Reprinted by
permission of Carol Mann Agency.
DAWN OF FREEDOM PUBLISHERS: Excerpt from "Mama Rose" by Archie
Shepp. Reprinted by permission of Dawn of Freedom Publishers.
NEW DIRECTIONS PUBLISHING CORPORATION: Excerpt from "This is Just to
Say" by William Carlos Williams from William Carlos Williams: *Collected
Poems Vol. I, 1909–1939*. Copyright 1938 by New Directions Publishing
Corporation. Reprinted by permission of New Directions Publishing
Corporation.

Library of Congress Cataloging-in-Publication Data
Odier, Daniel.
    [Baiser cannibale. English]
    Cannibal kiss: a novel/by Daniel Odier; translated by Lanie
Goodman.
        p.   cm.
    Translation of: Le baiser cannibale.
    ISBN 0-394-57595-4
    I. Title.
PQ2675.D5B313   1989
843'.914—dc20   89-42784

FOR NELL

"I want you to take this ex cannibal kiss
and turn it into a revolution!"

—*Archie Shepp, "Mama Rose"*

CANNIBAL KISS

"In the end, Bird, naked and painted in blue, slid open the door to the airplane and merged with the azure sky."

I had just put the final period to my novel. I felt transported into the void where I'd left my character floating. Outside my window spread the stark landscape that had given me the strength to go on until the end. The dunes and the beach, indifferent to my rage, solitude, despair, had not even spared the trace of my footsteps.

As if to prove to myself that the book hadn't obliterated me entirely, I stepped out into the icy air. It was dusk and the red line of the horizon enhanced the brilliance of the first stars. I stood up straight and stretched my spine. I walked down the sandy beach covered with tiny succulent plants. The oncoming darkness crackled with infinitesimal sounds. And then something happened that threw the book totally off course, and my life as well.

I know, the writer is supposed to keep himself at a reasonable distance from his work. He's supposed to be the deus ex machina. To pull the subtle strings of his marionettes. He's the conscientious architect, who knows every nook and cranny of the glass and steel palace that he's just constructed and, should the occasion arise, he's also there to reassure the reader and guide him toward the exit. But just imagine for a moment that the opposite occurs—that the flesh and blood of the author dissolves into the edifice, and that this edifice turns into a suspended and flexible bamboo structure, whose form is constantly changing . . .

Bird was traveling through space, she was merging with my desert and my book, lighter than the darkened sky. She was a fragment of azure and flesh, which I could hear moving through the atmosphere.

There was a sudden shock, a thud followed by the sound of something unfurling. Bird was hanging there suspended, slowly swinging back and forth, purple in her hair. My character had landed right inside my book, adding a parachute to my fiction, with no respect for her creator.

Bird rolled into the dust. The swelling nylon blisters had disappeared. She unfastened the straps of the parachute. The thick blue paint was furrowed with cracks.

Bird: "To quote one of your favorite writers: 'Art is an airplane that doesn't fly.' But I can fly, and I've come into your novel, into the world of the suffering writer. Dazai was right. Writers are pigs!"

I'd left Los Angeles the year before, mattress, records and books piled into my old Dodge. It was a long trip: five days all alone on the road. The bars, the desert in bloom, the tacky little motels, an emptiness that set in little by little.

Two days after my arrival in Pensacola, I'd tracked down the ideal place: a wooden shack in the dunes facing the ocean, lost in a lunar landscape.

A street lined with tall trees, bungalows in faded colors. Bird slams the door of a white house whose left side is caving in. She crosses a patio with a decrepit railing, past a junked Chevrolet that serves as a shelter for the neighborhood cats. Bird is walking fast. Her ferocity explodes into the warm air. The sound of television. Laughter floating through the night. A crushed bird on the grainy slab of asphalt.

"They call me Bird, like that bird, like Charlie Parker. I decided to commit suicide on the day of my fifteenth birthday. When the day arrived, I wasn't able to figure out how. There were too many possibilities. In the meantime, I decided to read a hundred books. The desire to die erases all fear."

Bird walks into Raj's house. Raj is a dealer from Pakistan. He's dozing in a hammock with a girl whose milky body is covered with freckles. Bird touches Raj's shoulder. His skin is the texture of a mango rind. His dark eyes hover in the night. Bird climbs into the hammock and lies down next to Raj. He takes her in his arms.

"Bird . . . what the hell are you doing in my hammock?"

"I'm listening to the crickets."

"You owe me twenty dollars."

"I need to borrow your motorcycle."

"The keys are on top of the TV."

"You're going to become 'café au lait' if you keep fucking that milkpail."

There's a steep path leading to a mobile home at the river's edge. The Indian, sprawled on a lounge chair, is eating fish and rice from a blackened pot. Distant, volatile, impenetrable, and always dressed in black leather. The Indian has only a first name, which he chose himself.

"You talk to the alligators?"

"I eat them. We haven't seen you in ages. You been reading Proust or something?"

"I can't get to sleep. It's been too hot."

"There's a bottle of pulque under your chair."

Bird takes a sip.

"I've always wondered if the worm at the bottom is still alive when they put it in the bottle."

"They're suicidal worms."

You could hear the swishing of rushes. A fish comes leaping up and gulps a little air. Screeching, grating jungle music.

"What I like most about Nature is the soundtrack."

Bird and the Indian are lying under a red paper Chinese umbrella that diffuses the light. The shadow of their bodies stretches before them.

"Did you register for the course with the new writer-in-residence?"

"Not yet."

"There's a short story of his in the *Village Voice,* there on the table."

"Is it good?"

Bird goes to look for the newspaper. The Indian falls asleep. The door of the trailer is still open. A slight breeze cools the atmosphere. Bird lies down on her stomach, kisses the Indian, and begins to read:

He watches the writer leave his house, get into his old Dodge and take off into the warm night toward the Blue Lagoon. Who is "he"? We'll call him the Chameleon, as Bird will later on, and say nothing more about it for the time being.

Walking up the red staircase, the writer inhales the odor of bodies, the sounds of reggae and his own smell. He walks across a long room lit by candles that have been placed in colored glasses. After a stop at the bar and a few glasses of rum, he lets himself go with the music.

Bird comes toward him. They dance for each other. Fusion, sudden attraction. By the time the musicians take a break they've told each other everything, except for a few details. Bird infects him with a blue-tinged malaria.

The writer sits on a bar stool. She rubs her back against him, swaying to the rhythm of the music. He caresses the nape of her neck, licks her brow, takes her in. She's wearing a black leather miniskirt and the remnants of a T-shirt. She turns around with a swivel of her hips. They smoke, drink, go outside. Even on Lincoln Boulevard you smell the ocean. Bird straddles her motorcycle and follows the writer's Dodge. There's something fragile about the sky. The light flickers.

The writer's apartment, on the third floor, opens onto a terrace shared by all the residents. They make themselves comfortable on the battered, slightly damp couch, exchange a little saliva and a few words that the Chameleon can't catch.

The apartment is almost empty, There's a mattress on the floor, some pillows, a black blanket. In front of the window is a door resting on trestles, used as a table. The writer leaves his clothes on the floor. Next to the bed, there's a stereo and a pile of books.

Daylight filtered into the apartment, finding their bodies intertwined on the bed, in the hallway, in every room, like a series of snapshots. They were gliding through space. At times they tried to pass through the walls. Little by little, the skin on their knees and elbows is worn away by the carpet. The sun is leaving its mark. The light is unbearable. They're under the table, exhausted. Finally, they get back into bed and bury their twisted bodies under the blanket.

So far it's nothing more than an ordinary encounter, the Chameleon thinks. Actually, he would have dozed off himself, just having emptied the fridge of some leftover tuna and a can of black olives, if Bird hadn't slid out of bed. The Chameleon looks at her body, marked by lovemaking, black and white in the ten o'clock morning sun. She pours herself a glass of milk and sits down in front of the typewriter. The Chameleon hears the uneven clicking of keys. He decides to go for a walk. He'll resume his post later on. He goes out, dancing to the rhythms of typography.

When he returns, he hears their cries. The writer is

beside himself. Bird, impassive, continues her writing. Looking out the bay window, the Chameleon counts thirteen palm trees. The writer gives full vent to his rage. Since Bird remains indifferent, he grabs her by the arm and drags her off her chair. He collects Bird's scanty clothes, flings them at her, and unceremoniously throws her out. The Chameleon is surprised by this unexpected display of violence, but he's seen it before. Now it's his turn to get into bed for a while. Observation is his passion, but he gets tired too, anyone would. He falls asleep, grateful for the darkness of the blanket that isolates him from the rest of the world.

When he awakes, the apartment is empty. The Chameleon goes downstairs. The motorcycle is gone. The Dodge isn't there either. What does the writer expect? he wonders, with a mocking smile. Does he think he can find Bird in a city like Los Angeles? It'll be even more difficult with the fog. Sides of buildings and fragments of palm trees suddenly emerge in a mercurial light. The Chameleon goes to buy the *Times* and settles down on the couch. He can hear the ocean without seeing it. Things were happening, as they always do. The Chameleon makes paper airplanes and amuses himself by throwing them off the terrace. The news disappears into the mist. The world has been emptied.

The writer returns alone, feeling tired. The Chameleon accompanies him to his apartment. Artists are strange. The writer rereads the thirty-odd pages, has a drink, looks for the tuna and olives in the refrigerator, and makes do with a cup of tea and a bag of cookies. He is pale and trembling. Maybe it's the light, the Chameleon thinks; he who, in general, is not easily alarmed. The only thing to do is to sleep until midnight.

The Blue Lagoon. The Chameleon had fallen asleep as well. Now, he arrives late. It must be two in the morning. The dance floor is so crowded that the Chameleon has a hard time finding the writer, who is dancing alone to get his mind off it all. The Chameleon takes a swig from his flask and meticulously screws it closed. He sits down on the corner of the stage and lets himself be entertained by the Jamaican musicians. A joint slides down to the bassist's feet. The Chameleon slips in between the musicians, lights the joint and returns to his outpost.

Through the ghostly mist, Bird suddenly appears. She's sitting at the bar. The writer hasn't seen her yet. She ends up joining him on the dance floor. Too much music for conversation. All that matters is to hold each other close. Or at least that's what the Chameleon imagines. They're the last ones to leave The Blue Lagoon. It's getting light outside. Comfortably sprawled in the back seat of the Dodge, the Chameleon can read the anguish mirrored on the writer's face. He's afraid that the motorcycle will disappear, and that Bird will take her book with her.

The typewriter clicks away. Bird still has her T-shirt on. Some African music is playing on the radio. The writer peels a mango and cuts it into slices. Between each paragraph, Bird swallows a few chunks. She drinks tall glasses of peach juice and coconut milk while the writer feverishly deciphers what she's written—it's exactly what he himself will write someday, in ten years or maybe twenty. He knows that these pages belong to him only. Bird is ephemeral.

Every morning on their way back from The Blue Lagoon, the writer goes to buy tropical fruit. Sometimes the Chameleon follows him. Otherwise he stays in the apartment with Bird, reading over her shoulder. He has a foreboding feeling. Why all this confusion? Was it really necessary to be trading dreams back and forth? What about solitude? He likes to watch them dance together. In fact, it's the part he likes the best. He could watch that day and night, but the days are set aside for artistic creation. Not to mention the writer is wearing himself out. Curled up under the blanket, full of desire for Bird, he lets her write for him. Those few hours during the night are his only moments of pleasure. Their liquid bodies fossilize at the break of day.

The Chameleon has no sense of time. It must be ten days and nights since Bird began writing.

Her eyes are red, her features drawn. She's getting thin, her breasts are losing their fullness. But it's when they're dancing that the Chameleon really starts to worry. Bird changes shape right before his eyes. Through some strange mimesis, she begins to resemble the writer.

For once, she's followed the writer into the shower. They have gone to lie down, their bodies dripping wet. The Chameleon seizes the opportunity to curl up in a corner of the living room. Their sighing and moaning keep him from falling into the deep sleep he so badly needs. It's unbearable for him, this sexual frenzy. The only thing he can do is drown it out with a steady stream of music. He turns on the radio and their bodies begin to dance lying down. Their cries turn into jungle music.

When he wakes up, the Chameleon realizes that once again it's too late for The Blue Lagoon. He drinks a little more coconut milk and notices that Bird and the writer are still asleep. The finished manuscript is stuck between their bodies. The dreaded moment. What will the writer do now?

They are talking to each other softly. The Chameleon notes how somber Bird's voice is. A shiver of pleasure runs down his spine. Even when she laughs, her tone of voice remains the same. The Chameleon listens and lets himself be rocked to sleep. The words don't matter to him.

What a celebration! She didn't stop talking all night. The Chameleon feels as though he's slept right on top of her black velvet vocal chords.

It's daybreak. He can see them a little better. The writer has dropped off to sleep. Bird kisses him, lulls him with indistinguishable words. She licks him, nibbles him, she begins to dance again in the profound silence of deep sucking.

It's getting lighter. There's practically nothing left of the writer. Just an imprint of a body on the mattress. Bird is dancing in the center of the white light. Her curves have returned. She's bursting at the seams. The perfume of her dripping body fills the room. The Chameleon blissfully inhales her scent. He's a little sorry that the writer has disappeared. It had been a pleasure following him. But he'd been so deliciously absorbed, you could only envy his final moments. That kind of disappearance is somewhat rare these days, when the hunger for one another takes on all kinds of disguises. The Chameleon tells himself that it's fair, even if the creator is consumed.

Even though Bird can't see him, the Chameleon feels as if she's dancing for him alone. She's offering him her voluptuous body.

By late afternoon, Bird has stopped dancing. She puts on her T-shirt and leather skirt and goes off to mail the writer's novel, after writing down the title on the yellow folder: *Cannibal Kiss.*

They went to sleep pressed against each other. Then, about three in the morning, the Chameleon gets on the back of the motorcycle. As they're riding off toward The Blue Lagoon, through the jasmine-scented night, he touches Bird's belly and thinks he feels something move. He probes her carefully. A little being was dancing inside her. There was no mistaking it. With his agile fingers the Chameleon positively identified the one who we'd have to call, with a certain affectionate derision, the writer.

Like every morning, the Indian is awakened by the noise of traffic on the highway. Bird is sitting on the bed, drinking coffee and watching him.

"What's going on? Did you sleep?"

"I was watching your beard grow."

"That's what you call eternity: a half of a millimeter per day."

The Indian pours himself some coffee. He lights a joint.

"She and I have the same name . . ."

"It's you. It's just that simple. That guy made you up."

The Chameleon hitchhikes as if it were the easiest thing in the world. He's decided to catch up with the writer. Going from one gas station to another, he steals potato chips, peanuts and bottles of soda. He chooses his ride carefully. He can't stand large families, or couples who take advantage of the monotonous trip to pour out their hearts, or the nuts with their blaring radios. He also avoids the farmers, who often take unexpected routes. Actually, nothing beats the trucks—long distances, steady speed, few stops, and the providential bed.

When he got to Pensacola, he caught a ride in a student's jeep. They drove alongside a stretch of ocean, through a pine forest, and arrived on campus. The Chameleon has a snack in the cafeteria and listens to the university radio station:

"We continue our evening of jazz with 'Lonely Woman' by Ornette Coleman, dedicated to our new writer-in-residence, the strange cannibal whom you can see in the flesh tonight, in Room 106 of the Comparative Literature Department. Don't miss this opportunity, there's still room to sign up. Cannibals, cannibals . . . I love 'em! Ah . . . I forgot. The name of the person who made this request . . . It's Bird, obviously."

The Chameleon can't help but smile. They have no idea what's in store for them. After a nap on the grass, the Chameleon wakes up just in time to find a seat in the back of the lecture hall. The writer is there, asking the students to check off their names on the computer listing. Then he takes out his Polaroid and starts taking pictures of them, group by group, so he will be able to recognize their faces more quickly. The students are whispering. They're talking about the writer, his jeans and black T-shirt with no inscription.

The Indian walks in and addresses the writer:

"I have a name, but I prefer to be called 'The Indian.'"

And suddenly, there she is, well, almost. An image of Bird, a variation, a budding blossom. Heat, humidity, perfume. The writer recognizes her. His body stiffens. Not because of her appearance, the leather miniskirt. This is more like a hallucination. The Chameleon is amused by the writer's uneasiness. Bird, delighted with her entrance, goes to sit in the first row. She wipes her brow and armpits with a tissue, crumples it into a ball and throws it in the wastepaper basket, at the writer's feet. He takes a picture of Bird. It doesn't feel like a class anymore. After a somewhat shaky introduction, his voice quivering ever so slightly, the writer begins to take Bird in. He wipes out all the other faces in the lecture hall. Only the Indian's presence resists obliteration.

Come here, I've been waiting for you. Write my book for me. I'll bring you mangoes, I'll lick you all over.

The Chameleon wonders who is spinning the web around whom. The Indian is savoring the emergence of each strand.

. . .

Her body is bulging with a future work. They dance to the music of words. The Chameleon comes closer to make sure he's not mistaken. Bird's body is already swaying, and the writer's is trembling.

The last part of the class is chaotic, on the verge of the incomprehensible. A nosedive toward the color of the sky. Nearly all the students have stopped taking notes. They're chasing after the words, seeking the meaning, the meaning. They'll have to get used to this sort of exercise.

The lecture hall is emptying out. The writer walks across the dark, balmy campus. Bird is just a few yards behind him.

"Thanks for 'Lonely Woman.'"

"Tomorrow it'll be 'Round Midnight.' It's Monk Month."

She laughs in the night.

ird and the Indian are parked under the trees along the river, across from the electric plant, bathed in a halo of pink light. They're having a smoke, hypnotized by the blinking reds and blues from the factory.

"Are you going to keep on doing this?"

"It's irreversible. The minute he saw me, I could tell that he knew I was Bird."

"Do you think he's the writer?"

"During the party, I saw that the latch on one of the windows was broken. Every night, he looks for me in the clubs people have told him about, and meanwhile I'm at his place. I get into his bed. I read everything. I lie down in his life. The letters from his agent are about a novel—an editor is interested in it, but so far there's nothing but fragments, unfinished beginnings, nothing. . . . Really nothing. The other night, I waited on the beach until he got home. I let him fall asleep and then I went in. I pulled back the black blanket and he was curled up in a ball, like a fetus . . . I got a good look at him. I felt a burning, something that was distorting his body, something you wouldn't notice when he's walking or dancing. It's what attracts me to him. And then there are these notes about me. I stick to his skin, I've become his obsession."

"I can see your white fangs growing in the dark."

"Words are the only thing I can give him."

"You'd disappear without words."

"Let's get out of here, I want to go dancing."

"You smell like paper, ink and death. I like that."

The Dodge is parked in front of a hangar. The Cubans use it as a shelter. The Indian and Bird go sit next to the writer, who's waiting for them in a dark corner. They finish a bottle of rum. The Indian is watching a film on the video screen.

"I want to be inside you."

"That would be difficult."

"Even for a hermaphrodite?"

"Show me . . ."

The three of them dance together. Later, they end up in a Puerto Rican woman's big wooden house. She feeds them rice, gumbo and dried bananas. The Indian falls asleep in his armchair.

Ladies and gentlemen, we are experiencing technical difficulties. Please stand by.

Now they're asleep. You can hear the ocean. The Chameleon opens the sliding doors that face out onto the beach. He finds Bird's skirt, then her T-shirt and the writer's clothes. Cautiously, he lifts up the black blanket and brushes aside Bird's dark hair to make sure that it's really her. Life is full of surprises.

He had set a character free and now he'd found her again. One should never lose patience. Yet, after the night at The Blue Lagoon, he'd really and truly lost her. Actually he'd found the writer again on another coast, but still.

Bird imprisons the writer in the dark flesh of her thighs and arms. The burns on her knees and elbows have healed. The Chameleon bends over Bird's body and inhales her. He's also discovered this, just like the writer. OK, now he has to decide. Will he stay with the writer or let himself get carried away by Bird?

Bird is five years old. She walks across the kitchen, climbs up onto a chair, concentrates for a moment, then jumps. She does this over and over before going on to the next step: the table. Her body touches ground in one graceful motion, barely making a sound.

Finally, she puts the chair on top of the table and leaps off the top of this improvised pyramid. She's becoming intoxicated by this succession of jumps. Her heart is beating very fast, her warmed muscles flex and stretch with lithe precision.

Lying on her bed, she tries to calm herself down. She concentrates on the rooftop pointing toward the sky.

Through the screen door of the bungalow, the Chameleon watches a woman who's about fifty years old. The superimposed layers of pain and alcohol have created a mask of indifference.

With a can of beer in her right hand and a cigarette between the thumb and forefinger of her left, she brings them both to her lips, one after the other in an unalterable rhythm, but never takes her eyes off the blue and pink images on the old TV set. The volume is turned up, full of static.

Bird walks into the kitchen. The Chameleon takes advantage of the open door of the refrigerator to grab himself a can of Coke. Bill, who's about forty, thin, red-eyed, with disheveled hair and grease-stained hands, is making spaghetti. Bird turns down the TV.

Bill: "Are you hungry?"

Bird: "I've already eaten. Don't you think it smells like gas in here?"

Bill: "I've got to get another stove."

Bird: "Open the window, I don't feel like getting blown up."

The Chameleon's mouth is watering. He's hoping they'll give him a chance to taste the sauce, which has a subtle aroma composed of olive oil, garlic, thyme, black pepper, meat and tomatoes. That's the problem when you're invisible—people don't always remember you're there.

Bill: "It's hot as hell."

He looks at the postcards tacked on the wall. He takes one off. It's a picture of a motel. He turns it over to read the message:

Dear Sassy, I got a job in Detroit. I'll send you a little money. Give my love to Bird. Let me know how you are. I think I'll be staying in this motel for a few months.

John

Another card: the ocean, a beach, and some palm trees.

You're a couple of bitches. Glad I got the hell out. Life is livable.

Roy

Dallas, the highways, downtown:

I guess I should never have left. Do you always know what you're doing when you're doing it? I once read an article where the guy claimed you do. I needed a change of atmosphere but now I'm lonely. Maybe I'll be back someday.

Love, Ron

Bill: "I never understood why Sassy keeps these post-cards . . ."

Bird tastes the spaghetti.

Bird: "They keep her company."

Bill: "What for? I'm here . . ."

Bird: "One day, there'll be nothing left of you but an old pair of jeans, a razor, and a pair of sneakers that I'll throw in the garbage. So then Sassy can reread the postcards."

Bill: "Why are you telling me this? You know how much I love you."

Bird: "I love you a lot too, Bill, but the time will come when you won't be able to take all this anymore, just like the rest of them. You'll send us a couple of cards, they'll become part of the collection, and then you'll be forgotten, like I've forgotten about eighty percent of my 'fathers.' I've always thought that I must have been born from a sperm cocktail."

Bill: "We'll see . . . How's it going at the university?"

Bird: "I'm going to quit so I can do some research."

Bill: "Research on what?"

Bird: "Something literary. A writer is going to give me a little money."

The Chameleon gulps down a handful of spaghetti, then a spoonful of sauce. This Bill knows what he's doing. Must be Italian.

Sassy gets up for a can of beer from the refrigerator. The light shines on her face, puffy from alcohol.

Bill: "D'ya hear that, Sassy?"

Sassy: "Uh . . . Research . . . Something literary . . ."

Sassy sits back down. Bird sets the table. Bill serves.

The Chameleon follows Bird into her room: it's the size of a matchbox. There's a typewriter sitting on a folding card table. Bird rolls herself a joint, puts on the record "Out Front," Booker Little, Eric Dolphy and Max Roach. She stretches out on her red nylon sleeping bag. The Chameleon takes a look at the books—each one represents a different moment of respite, a new flight. Like Bird, he lets himself go with the music, lying peacefully by her side, inhaling a little smoke as it goes by. Bird's clothes are hanging on a wire. In the cardboard box is a collection of strange hats. During the middle of the night, a tiger-striped cat jumps onto the windowsill. The presence of the Chameleon makes him hesitate a moment, but he finally curls up to sleep between them.

Bird is naked. She stretches and opens her eyes. The cat settles down between her breasts.

"I'd love to take you with me, Mr. Lester Young, but it's going to be a dog's life."

Bird gets up and slips on a T-shirt and panties. She feeds the cat and makes some coffee and toast, which she covers with butter and honey. Lester Young comes to lap up his milk.

After contemplating herself in the mirror above the sink, Bird decides to cut her hair very short. One after the other, she throws the locks of hair into a garbage bag, then heads for the shower next to the kitchen.

When she comes out, draped in a blue towel, Bill and Sassy are in the middle of breakfast. They look at Bird with surprise.

Bill: "You should have cut it all off."

Bird: "Did you drink all the coffee?"

Bill: "There wasn't any left. No more toast, either."

Sassy: "We're going to the lake. You want to come?"

Bird: "I'm leaving this morning."

Sassy: "For how long?"

Bird: "Six months, maybe more."

Sassy: "Do you have any money?"

Bird: "A little."

Sassy: "How much do we have, Bill?"

Bill: "About one thousand three hundred."

Sassy: "Give her two hundred."

Bill goes to get the money.

Sassy: "I don't ask much of you."

Bird: "I'll give you a call every now and then."

The Chameleon puts the novel he'd been avidly reading back where it was. Bird takes her sleeping bag and a few items of carefully selected clothing and stuffs them in a duffle bag. She gathers together her jazz cassettes, slips on her leather skirt and boots, puts on her sunglasses and an orange silk hat that looks a lot like the one that Monk is wearing on the cover of one of his albums. The Chameleon is very excited. It feels like a grand departure. At the last minute, he makes up his mind and steals a beret, which gives him an entirely authentic bebop look.

Bird and Bill kiss each other good-bye.

Bill: "Take care of yourself."

Bird: "Be good to Sassy."

Sassy is sitting in bed, sobbing. Bird takes her in her arms.

Bird: "Everything will be all right."

The Chameleon turns on the TV. Life must go on.

Sassy and Bill watch her go. It's autumn.

A river of watery blue flows into the gray-shadowed sky. The tornado is approaching the city. The blue stream is twisting, striking as it advances. Trucks are flying, cars are piling up, roofs and sides of houses are being carried away, bits and pieces of life are gliding past. The trees bend, resistant to being uprooted.

Suddenly, a calm descends on the ravaged city.

Sassy, haggard, stands in front of the empty cradle caught among the branches of a red maple.

"Bird!"

had walked on the beach until I was drunk with exhaustion. My legs were trembling, I was saturated with salty air. A writer ready for anything so he won't have to write. Solitude, anguish, waiting. The acid songs of the night birds. Mockery, that elusive phantom.

I sat down on the wooden planks of the terrace. The Indian had the memory of Bird, Bird had space. I asked myself why the hell I was obsessed with blackening a white page. Little by little, the incessant pounding of the waves drained me of my emotions.

I thought about the mailbox. The first message from Bird was waiting for me inside a big floppy envelope.

The weather was disgusting when I left town and it took me fifteen hours to get to Memphis. I'm in a motel. I'm being watched by a stag who's got the face of a politician. He's surrounded by a snowy landscape. Who in the world could paint such crap? When animals begin to look like we do, it gives me the creeps. I think of the years he must have spent listening to human conversations, watching TV or couples climbing on top of each other. So I closed his eyes with a felt pen. Ever since then, he began to forget. He's losing his human expression.

You know how stubborn the smell of a cheap motel

can be. Old rotting carpet, the heat. I've got the fan on.
A kid dressed in a sari brought me a plate of chicken curry.
Then she came back and put some kohl on my eyelids.

The TV picture is as blurry as an Impressionist painting. It's an old RCA with a radio. I found a jazz station
and now I'm lying on the damp bed. I'm sending you a
pillowcase that I rubbed on my belly. You have to get your
kicks somehow! If you want to feel like an American, just
stick the pillowcase over your head, cut some eyeholes, and
go take a stroll in a black neighborhood. I thought of that
because I just heard "Strange Fruit."

Kindly accept my most deliriously fevered regards.

Bird

The Indian didn't come to class. I spent the night going back and forth from the hangar, to one house after another, to music clubs, caught in a sort of trance. No one had seen him.

Around six in the morning, I sat down on one of his lounge chairs. I drank some tequila. The Indian came out of the river, naked.

"I thought there were alligators in there."

"Water snakes and all kinds of other creatures. Maybe alligators, who knows?"

"I brought some money for Bird."

The Indian went into his trailer, put on a pair of pants, then came over to sit next to me.

"She saw blue tire tracks on the highway. Then the tracks stopped all of a sudden. I think she left Memphis. I don't know where she's going."

"I wish she'd leave me a phone number sometimes."

"I doubt if she will. I'll be in class next week. This week I had some problems. I lost fifteen thousand dollars in the stock market."

"Fifteen thousand dollars?"

"Oil. My family lives on a reservation in Oklahoma. The government pays dividends to the whole tribe. That's what we live on. I'm the one who takes care of investing the money.

Which is how I can afford a car, to rent this room, and on top of it all, go to school."

"Have you known Bird a long time?"

"We met at the hospital. She'd fractured her ankle, and I'd been in a car accident. She was fifteen, I was eighteen. That crazy thing she has about jumping."

"Jumping?"

"She's always done it. I don't know where she got the idea. She's had five or six accidents. That's why I nicknamed her Bird."

"Is it her name?"

"She didn't wait for you to invent her so she could exist. I can even tell you that she existed for real long before I met her. At that time, she was still in high school."

The Indian gets up, puts on a shirt and lights a joint.

"Pure Caribbean."

"We could almost swim there."

"Just about. Every now and then, a Cuban and some sugar cane get washed up on shore, sometimes some containers of smack, too. But further north."

A little crescent of a moon was making ripples on the water. We listened.

"Ever since she was little, she's been practicing how to jump. From higher and higher up. That's why her legs and ass are like steel. I've seen her throw herself off the second story of a house. Once she gets it into her head, there's no stopping her. Even dope hasn't replaced this obsession with traveling through space. That's what fascinated me when we were at the hospital together. She'd barely got out when she started to do it all over again, little by little. You see that tree there? She jumped from the lowest branches. A year later, she threw herself off the very top."

B ird is having a bowl of chili in a fast food restaurant.

Most of the rocks at the base of the Sea of Tranquility are covered with little holes of a diameter of a few millimeters. These holes are mini-craters drilled by the impact of tiny meteorites, smaller than the head of a pin. These minuscule particles strike the surface of the moon at a speed that can exceed 100,000 kilometers per hour: a point at which energy is acquired that, in equal weight, exceeds an explosion of TNT. Every day billions of particles of this size enter the earth's atmosphere, but friction burns them up before they reach the sun. They disintegrate in the atmosphere and then leave behind them incandescent traces known as "shooting stars."

The Chameleon has been following Bird ever since she left. The icy wind sends a strip of orange cellophane flying between the buildings. Bird has been following the monster since nightfall. The first time she passed him was when she was coming out of the movies. Instantly she was fascinated by the albino's animal-like face. His body spills out over a pair of gray work pants. Despite the cold, he's wearing nothing but a T-shirt and you can see patches of pink skin through the holes. There's a small spark flickering in his incandescent eyes. He trudges along, pushing a shopping cart from the supermarket, in which is a plastic jug. He stops every now and then to take a drink. Bird catches a stream of sounds, an unintelligible language.

The albino comes to a halt and props his cart up on the curb. Limber despite his deformity, he sits down, tucking his knees under his chin and clasping the jug tightly. The sound he's making seems more like an invitation than a moan. Bird comes closer. The albino fishes around in his pocket, takes out a Zippo lighter, flicks it and in the glimmer of the flame notices Bird, who is now very near. He looks only vaguely curious.

"You want me to give you a ride?"

Bird starts pushing the cart. The albino doesn't object. At the next intersection, he holds out his right arm, like a cyclist, to show which way he wants to go. Bird follows his directions.

They arrive in front of an old thirties' hotel, with all of its entrances boarded up. Guided by the albino, Bird finally discovers a sliding plank in back of the hotel, at the end of an alley. The albino gets out of the cart and puts it in a safe spot. They slip the wooden panel back into place. Deserted corridors, ice-cold. Red peeling wallpaper. They walk through the former lobby. Sitting motionless on a counter, a rat watches them.

The albino pauses between each flight to catch his breath. Finally, they reach the top of the building. The albino pushes open the door of Room 2356, lights a candle and Bird sinks into one of the armchairs. The albino heats up some water and pours it into a cup, which he holds out to Bird. One wall is covered with discount coupons. The albino hunts through a pile of clothes and finds a coat that he drapes over Bird's shoulders. He sits down in a corner of the room on a piece of blue foam rubber that he uses as a bed. He drinks as he watches Bird, takes a little radio out of his pocket and tries to find some music. The crackling sound of Brazilian music fills the room. The albino's body starts to move to the rhythm. He stands up. His movements are almost graceful. Soon he starts making little hoarse, rhythmic noises. He stops, carefully chooses a few coupons which he gives to Bird, and goes back to dancing. Bird gets up to dance for the albino, who is watching her as he continues to wiggle the flaccid bulk of his body.

Bird slips on the coat and sits down on the piece of foam rubber. She takes the albino's hand and caresses it. He contemplates her with his milky gaze, relaxes, turns over on his side and snuggles up next to Bird, curled into the shopping-cart position. Bird strokes his white hair and his face. The albino is making a sustained husky purring sound. When the radio shuts off by itself, he gets a little nervous, moves around. In a deep voice, Bird starts to sing anything that comes to mind. Pleased, the albino goes back to his old position. Bird notices that he has six fingers on his left hand, short and slender little fingers attached to an extremely large palm.

The next morning, Bird wakes up beside the albino, who's watching her while he polishes his lighter with a sock. The minute she opens her eyes, he boils water to cook some eggs.

He brings Bird into the room next door, where the carpet is covered with dried turds, all carefully lined up. He's anxious for Bird to add one to the collection, after which he'll also relieve himself, continuing the line of these square grids. He shows Bird about twenty other rooms decorated the same way.

The sun filters through the dusty windows. The albino pushes Bird's chair into a ray of light. Slowly, she begins to warm up and blows her nose into a piece of paper. The albino holds out his hand, imitates her gesture, carefully folds up the sheet of paper and pins it in the center of a bare wall. Then he opens the closet, looks around for a magazine, opens it to a photo of an ocean liner and drops it into Bird's lap.

They walk into a restaurant. Bird orders some pie, chili, hot dogs, and coffee. The waitress can't take her eyes off the albino, who's indifferently dousing his hot dog with ketchup, covering it with a thick layer of condiments. He eats slowly, closing his eyes from time to time. Bird gets up, goes over to the juke box and selects some songs. The albino is emptying packets of saccharine on his tongue and washing it all down with a cup of coffee.

"Do you know Al?" the waitress asks Bird.

"I met him yesterday."

"You're not afraid of him?"

"Has he lived here for a long time?"

"They call him Al. I always see him hanging around. He comes by for the leftovers when the boss isn't here."

The heart-shaped Jacuzzi and big brass bed were lit up by pink spotlights. Bird gets undressed and sinks into the boiling water. The albino looks on hesitantly, then joins her. He floats, dives, reemerges and disappears, a little pink whale. Bird is fascinated by the ease with which his body moves underwater.

The bus lets them off across from the ocean. Despite the fact that it's winter, Al takes off his clothes and throws himself into the water. Huddled in her jacket, Bird watches him rise up from the waves, vanish beyond the breaking-point of the surf, then effortlessly come back toward shore. Al won't get out of the water until late afternoon, his skin purple.

·   ·   ·

They spend the night dancing in a reggae club, go to a deli for supper, where Al devours a couple of pastrami sandwiches, then go back to Bird's motel. Al spends several hours in the shower before going to sleep, and doesn't get up until the middle of the next afternoon.

As soon as they set foot in the Center of Oceanography, where the young hammerhead sharks are playing in an immense blue aquarium, Al starts to make little squealing sounds and shake all over. He goes up to the glass partition and presses his entire body against it. He's holding on to Bird's hand. When the Center is ready to close, Bird has a hard time convincing Al that he's got to leave.

Now they're heading toward a big Gothic-style house made of wood. Bird allows herself to be led, still soaked from all those hours of dancing. It'll be light out soon.

It's a schoolroom. On the wall is a big map of the ocean floor, with peaks and mountain ranges buried under the deep blue. The albino is sitting on a desk. His huge body sways back and forth on the creaking wood. Bird is seeing the world upside-down, a reflection of Al's milky profile. Albino Al, the last white whale.

A bird cemetery in the Louisiana jungle. Bird, her bag slung over her shoulder, blazes a trail for herself. The fragile bones make a dry crunching sound under her feet.

She looks for a tree that's high enough and one that she'll be able to climb. Then she squats down, digs into her bag, and pulls out the photos of Parker, Monk, and Dolphy. Using her hands, she buries them at the base of the tree among the other birds. After a moment of concentration, she gazes at the top of the tree, undresses, and nimbly works her way up.

Poised precariously on a limb, she looks down at the birds' remains and jumps.

Bird is sitting by the ocean in New Orleans. Her left leg is in a cast.

The bulging envelope was light. It contained bulbs of raw cotton and a sonnet by Shakespeare recopied in Bird's own writing. The envelope had been mailed in Tennessee.

> In the old age black was not counted fair,
> Or if it were, it bore not beauty's name;
> But now is black beauty's successive heir,
> And beauty slander'd with a bastard shame:

For since each hand hath put on Nature's power,
Fairing the foul with Art's false borrow'd face,
Sweet beauty hath no name, no holy bower,
But is profan'd, if not lives in disgrace.
Therefore my mistress' brows are raven black,
Her eyes so suited, and they mourners seem
At such who, not born fair, no beauty lack,
Sland'ring creation with a false esteeem:
Yet so they mourn, becoming of their woe,
That every tongue says beauty should look so.

The Chameleon is close enough for Bird to sense his presence. Sometimes she thinks she sees his reflection in a shop window. At night, she can hear him breathing.

The Chameleon isn't too fussy. He accepts the conditions that Bird has imposed during the trip. What he's really interested in is Bird's inner thoughts. He couldn't care less about crossing deserts, waiting for the bus that never comes, sleeping anywhere possible, or catching a ride in any car that comes along.

One night, Bird looks in a mirror. The white glare of public toilets in a train station. Suddenly, she has the fleeting impression that her face is sliding into a void. Her features are moving so fast that her eyes, nose and mouth look as though they'd been covered with clear plastic bags. Bird puts her dark glasses and hat back on, then she goes to the post office to collect the writer's money that the Indian has been sending her regularly.

Outside, the Chameleon melts into the landscape, he disappears into the walls, he takes on the colors of the sky, of the asphalt streets, of the night.

Bird walks into a stadium where several thousand spectators are taking their seats for a football game between two teams of black giraffe-women, completely naked except for their helmets—red for the Atlanta team, blue for the one from Chicago. Bird, the only white woman in the stadium, is sitting in the first row. After the parades of majorettes accompanied by a brass band, the eleven players of each team make their entrance from the north and south doors of the stadium. The crowd begins to cheer.

A scrimmage. The kickoff. The giraffe-women run very fast, supported by legs which by minimum standards must be at least five feet long. Their airy, long-legged strides elicit cries of admiration from the crowd. Very soon, the ebony of their athletic bodies is beaded with sweat. Their abnormally strained muscles glisten. Their hard breasts dance in rhythm. Leaps into space. The violent impact of the ball being intercepted. They're tumbling down—another kickoff at lightning speed. Bird can hear one of the players panting as she streaks past her. The moves are so unpredictable and rapid that the ball sails through the sky as if it were in slow motion. The TV cameramen are having a hard time keeping up with them; even the commentators are lost, since not one player is wearing a number. There are only glistening bodies, almost silver under a dark sky of ashen clouds. The sparkle in their eyes shines right through the grids of the helmets. The players are screaming, falling down, getting back up. It's becoming difficult to count the goals scored by each team.

Suddenly, the match is over. It's a tie.

One woman from the red team and another from the blue team take off their helmets. There is silence in the stadium. You can hear the sound of their bare feet crushing the blades of grass. The closer they get, the more Bird is fascinated by their dripping bodies, their slow, heavy breathing.

The two giraffe-women come to a halt just a few yards away from Bird, who freezes for an instant.

Then she rises, approaches the giraffe-women determinedly, and, in the silence, begins to lick them.

I t's a nude by Man Ray. Bird has written on top of it in silver ink:

> This sentence makes me burst into tears. Why? *He wants to help Angel kill the alligators.*

A freight train pulls into the station in Kansas City. Bird, who's twelve years old, slides open the door of a cattle car. The train comes to a standstill. She looks around, hops out, and runs between the tracks, avoiding the towering shadow of the station.

It is very early. The sky is a deep blue. Bird gazes at the buildings downtown. The city is almost deserted.

Bird buys a bottle of milk, some cheese, a loaf of bread and some mustard. She has only a few dollars in her pocket. She crosses the parking lot and sits down in the sun. She produces a pocketknife from her bag, slices a piece of cheese, covers it with mustard, and puts it on a piece of bread.

Bird eats and drinks. She watches the people go by, their shopping carts overflowing with food.

It's nighttime. Bird crosses a highway, the glare of headlights silhouetting her profile. She enters a park, looks around for a place to sleep. She wraps herself in a blanket, opens her knife and sticks it in the ground.

A black man about fifty years old passes by, humming to himself. Noticing Bird, he goes over to her, pauses a moment to watch her sleep, then shakes her.

The Black Man: "Hey, little girl . . . what are you doing here? It's dangerous at night."

Bird wakes with a start, grabs her knife and quickly recoils. The black man laughs.

The Black Man: "Put that away, I'm not going to hurt you."

Bird: "Get the hell out of here!"

The Black Man: "You ran away from home, didn't you?"

Bird: "Fuck off!"

The Black Man: "If you say so, but you'll be picked up by tomorrow morning. Let's just hope it'll be by the cops."

Bird calms down a bit.

Bird: "I'm holding on to my money for food."

The Black Man: "Come and sleep at my place, you'll be better off."

He offers her a cigarette and lights one for himself as well. Bird is silent. She takes a few puffs, looks at the man, smokes some more, throws down the cigarette, puts her knife in her pocket and packs up her blanket.

Bird: "OK, let's go."

Joe, his wife, Nina, and Bird are in the kitchen eating waffles.

Joe: "You should've seen her with her knife. A real spit-fire."

Nina: "She's absolutely right. You never know who you're

dealing with. Your parents must be worried. Don't you want to give them a call?"

Bird: "I'll be going home in a few days."

Joe: "You know we can't let you stay here, we'd have to let your family know where you are."

Bird: "Just give me three days to wander around. I'll come back here to sleep."

Nina: "All right. But then we're putting you on a Greyhound."

Joe and Bird pull up in front of a little movie house from the thirties called The Gem. Joe's driving an old black Buick.

They walk into the cinema and then go up to the projection booth. Joe sets up a reel.

Joe: "Why don't you go sit down there, you'll be more comfortable."

Bird: "No, I'm staying here with you."

The water, streaked with every imaginable shade of green, reflects the stifling heat. Blue and red birds dart through the air, which is filled with all sorts of hissing and scraping noises, cries, mating calls; thick and muted sounds that hit you in the gut and make you tingle all the way down to your fingertips. A boat glides through the odors of resin, the carnivorous flowers, the dozing tigers. A young girl standing in the bow plants her pole in the water and suddenly drives the boat forward. She's singing in a charming and incomprehensible language that she's just made up. The alligators are watching her from behind the rushes.

The ship's prow slides over the black sand. The young girl jumps out onto the riverbank. She forges a path through the jungle. The reptiles lick her feet with their rose and silvery forked tongues, feet that are deep blue in color like the rest of her body.

received a letter from Bird written between the lines of a page torn from a book:

woods, even in common nights, than most suppose. I
I wonder what kind of weird desire makes you try to reach into the
frequently had to look up at the opening between the trees
darkest depths of my being. Who's giving the Lesson of Darkness to
above the path in order to learn my route, and where there was
whom? You dreamed of becoming some kind of quicksand that would
no cart-path, to feel with my feet the faint track which I had
suck me in, but I'm the one who's going to slide myself right into you.
worn, or steer by the known relation of particular trees which
I'm going to change the rules of the game. I don't give a shit about
I felt with my hands, passing between two pines for instance,
your list. I'll trust my instincts. Don't worry, you won't be disap-
not more than eighteen inches apart, in the midst of the woods,
pointed. I received your money. I'll send you a tape soon. There's
invariably, in the darkest night. Sometimes, after coming home
something disgusting about you that attracts me and something
thus late in a dark and muggy night, when my feet felt the path
almost clean that revolts me. Unless of course you're some kind of
which my eyes could not see, dreaming and absent-minded all
genius that I'm making up as I go along. We'll see. For now I'll just
the way, until I was aroused by having to raise my hand to lift
explore, look, touch, feel, lick, taste, learn, listen, observe, forget,

the latch, I have not been able to recall a single step of my walk,

laugh, cry, suffer, enjoy, roam around, disappear, elude your gaze

and I have thought that perhaps my body would find its way

and disappear. There's a part of me inside that gets harder and

home if its master should forsake it, as the hand finds its way

harder, darker and darker, floating under the transparency of my

to the mouth without assistance. Several times, when a visitor

skin. I guess these are the precious tidbits you'd like to have in your

chanced to stay into evening, and it proved a dark night, I was

mouth so you can suck on the black crystals. What the hell are you

obliged to conduct him to the cart-path in the rear of the house,

doing all alone in that dump on the beach? Great surges of adolescent

and then point out to him the direction he was to pursue, and

mysticism must be burning out your brain. Night, day, the obsession

in keeping which he was to be guided rather by his feet than his

to write this book, to carry on until the very end, to escape all forms

eyes. One very dark night, I directed thus on their way two

and constraints, to this supposed freedom you've been drilling into us,

young men who had been fishing in the pond. They lived about

this freedom that I've already got and that stabs you like a sword. An

a mile off through the woods, and were quite used to finding

artist is a miser, an able creature, dedicated to unfulfillment, to

the route. A day or two after one of them told me that they

eternal dissatisfaction, to suffering. I live for every moment. But what

wandered about the greater part of the night, close to their own

about you? I've learned a few things. Get ready to suffer in silence

premises, and did not get home till around morning, by which

when my lips are near you, get ready to be torn apart, get ready for

time, as there had been several heavy showers in the meanwhile,

disintegration, get ready to forget writing it'll melt in my mouth, the

and the leaves were very wet, they were drenched to their skins.

words will dissolve, become unrecognizable. There'll be no more lan-
I have heard of many going astray even in the village streets,
when the darkness was so thick that you could cut it with a
knife, as the saying is. Some who live in the outskirts, having
come to town a-shopping in their wagons have
guage, no more words. Bites . . . Bird

"I have a strange nose. . . . The more I look at it, the stranger it gets."

"Why do writers hang on like blind monkeys to the idea that sex, orgasms, are linked to death?"

"What are you talking about?"

"The Indian and I are trying to have a conversation."

"Stories about noses are fascinating. . . . Now there's a great conversation piece. A thousand times better than your stupid-ass ideas."

"It's a religious concept, it's cultural residue, a pale Puritan perception, a confusion between death and the void. There's no such thing as spermatozoa rushing toward death—it's only in the heads of those guys brought up in the convent. . . . You know how it is. . . . All it takes is for one great writer to say something fucking stupid and it'll be passed along from century to century like some kind of precious gift. Just imagine those poor guys racking their brains, thinking that their peckers were diddling around in the cavern of death. Ha ha!"

"Yeah, I can understand that. Yeah . . . sure. It's something that's always bugged me, but it's more ingrained in people's minds than God is. OK . . . well . . . but, then what isn't linked to death, huh?"

"Instead of knocking your brains out with your dumb

stories, you should try examining my nose. You could touch it, make it the subject of a lecture, a colloquium, a symposium . . ."

"Breathing isn't linked to death."

"Stop breathing, you two!"

"So what isn't linked to death?"

"Only death itself. . . . In my opinion . . .

"Who was it again who wrote a whole story about a nose that moves around all by itself?"

"Gogol. Wasn't it Gogol?"

"Uh . . . Gogol. . . . Yeah. . . . Gogol and Poe. Poe's story goes like this: 'The first action of my life was the taking hold of my nose with both hands.'"

"Wow, what a beginning!"

"In my opinion, but I could be wrong—in my opinion— let's finish this bottle—in my opinion, the Ideal would be . . ."

"Who's talking about ideals in my house? Who's the bastard who used that word?"

"Keep your nose out of it, Victoria. You're sucking us dry!"

"It's your conversation that sucks!"

"The Ideal would be to refute the arguments of all those who believe in being, of all those who believe in non-being, and those who don't believe in either being or non-being . . ."

"And all those who contest the usefulness of handkerchiefs."

"Are you coming, Indian? I have a friend who just cooked some feijoada . . . sound tempting?"

"And how."

"OK, let's get out of here."

"Would you cut the bullshit! I'm the one who invited you for feijoada, remember? Can't you smell it? It's been simmering on the stove for hours. Let's eat!"

B ird is crossing Death Valley. The Chameleon remains on top of the ridge. From time to time, he can make out the tiny silhouette below, lost in the red mist. Rays of evening light.

> Eagle touched down on the surface of the Sea of Tranquility on July 20, 1969, at 4:18 P.M. E.D.T. "The surface is fine and powdery," Armstrong said. "I can pick it up loosely with my toe. It does adhere in fine layers like powdered charcoal to the sole and sides of my boots. I can only go in a small fraction of an inch. Maybe an inch, but I can see the footprints of my boots and the treads in the fine sandy particles." Armstrong's boots sank in six or seven inches in some places. The Armstrong footprints will remain clearly visible for ten million years.

A motorboat passes through a series of lagoons bordered with lush vegetation. Bird is sitting up front, and a Puerto Rican is steering the boat. Alligators slink between the rushes.

They moor at a landing, Bird takes her bag, steps out. She's wearing black sunglasses and her beret. The Puerto Rican signals to her to walk all the way to the middle of the island. A path choked by the jungle, birds taking flight. The boat is moving off in the distance. There's only the silence, broken by cries. Bird makes her way deeper into the jungle.

She reaches a warehouse. An old man, Ricardo, tall and very thin, is sitting on a stool in the shade of the porch playing a shakuhachi, a long Japanese flute of lacquered bamboo. Bird comes closer, stops, and listens until Ricardo puts the flute down on his lap. He scrutinizes Bird silently.

Bird: "I brought you an instrument."

Ricardo: "I have every instrument in the world. I've spent my life at it. As you've heard, I only show my collection to those who come to give me a piece that I don't already have."

Bird: "You couldn't possibly have the instrument I brought you."

Ricardo: "Show it to me."

Bird: "No."

Ricardo: "Go jump in the lagoon with the alligators!"

Ricardo picks up his shakuhachi again and starts to play. Bird sits on the ground.

Ricardo puts his flute on the stool, disappears into the warehouse and comes back with a wheelchair with straps attached to it. He motions for Bird to get into it. He straps her in, first her legs, then her arms. He ends up by wrapping a collar around her throat, then takes off her glasses and blindfolds her with the scarf he's wearing around his neck.

He pushes the wheelchair inside the hangar. There's a kitchen, a room full of books. Now they're going into the real hangar itself. Ricardo disappears into a little shack with dead-bolt locks on the doors; he closes the door behind him.

The ride continues. He subjects Bird to a tortuous route, as he winds around the instruments. The hangar is completely empty, bathed in the rays coming through the panes of the skylight. Ricardo steers around the scattered rectangular patches of light.

You could hear the sounds of every instrument Ricardo was naming: a bone flute from the Stone Age, a quena, an African flute, an ujusini, a metal flute, a reed shepherd's-pipe, a shakuhachi, a necklace of flutes made from the bones of Panamanian birds, an Aztec tlapitztali, a flute of clay . . .

"Tell me what you're hiding!"

An Indian flute, a jazzo flute, a tin whistle, a cuckoo whistle, a schrillpfeife, a picco pipe, a galoubet, a txistu, a bosco whistle . . .

"Is it a wind instrument?"

A Maori nguru, a cipactli, a shiwaya, an ombgwe, a khumbgwe, a nightingale whistle, an ocarina, a ti-tzu, a fuye, a naka ya lethlake, a fife without keys, a fife with keys, a Polynesian nose flute, a double flute, a triple flute . . .

"Is it a percussion instrument?"

A Tibetan gling-bu, a dvojacka, a quadruple flute, a panpipe, a p'ai hsio, a baroque flute, a bass, tenor, alto, soprano, and sopranino recorders, double-bass, a flageolet, a four-key ivory flute, a bamboo flute, a sword flute, a glass flute, a simple idioglottal clarinet, a heteroglottal clarinet, a bumpa, horn pipes, a tiktiri, a diplesurle, a diplice, a double clarinet, an urua, a launeddas, an arghul, a zummara, a double clarinet of bird bone, a bass, tenor, alto, and soprano set of pipes, a clarinet in E-flat, in B-flat, in A, an alto, bass and contrabass clarinet . . .

"I'm telling you, I've got everything! Devoted my life to it! All my passion! Even the strangest sounds! Cries of animals, the songs of whales, the hissing of sorcerers, incantations, secret murmurings . . ."

A string bass, a basset horn, a love clarinet, a tarogato, a tenor saxophone, a soprano saxophone, an octavin, a zurla, a sopile, a surnaj, a tiple, a bombarde, a sona, a sralay, a pi naï, a crumhorn . . .

Bird: "Undo these straps!"

Ricardo stops and looks around the hangar while the instruments continued to resonate all by themselves.

Bird: "Too bad. You'll never know."

Ricardo: "I can search through your things."

Bird: "You won't find it."

Ricardo leaves Bird where she is, goes to get her bag and returns. Bending over it, he takes everything out, then examines the compartments, the lining, and the sleeping bag. He takes a pen apart and blows into the barrel.

Ricardo: "That's it!"

Bird: "No it isn't."

He unstraps Bird. She rises and walks through the hangar without undoing her blindfold. She's trying to sense the presence of the instruments, but encounters only empty space.

Bird concentrates; her body stretches upward, suddenly contracts, then expands with her slow, deep breathing.

The sound of her cry fills the hangar.

A short message, scrawled in blue crayon on a white card:

> Did you know that in certain African tribes, they believe in the concept of the female father? A woman of royal birth marries a female servant, then chooses a man for her. The noblewoman is considered thereafter the father of the couple's child.
>
> Bird

Bill and Sassy are having dinner in the kitchen.

Sassy: "Did I ever tell you the story about how Bird was born?"

Bill: "I don't remember."

Sassy: "It was when they were trying out all kinds of new stuff. You could choose between giving birth in the water, with acupuncture, or squatting down like the Indians. I went for the last one. The doc had lowered the lights. It was in a blue room . . . deep blue . . . But I wasn't really squatting, I was hovering in the air over some sort of machine, and it took forever, she didn't want to come out. The doctor and nurses were discussing the best way to drive on the highway. They were having an argument about whether it was better to overinflate your tires or underinflate them, when all of a sudden Bird came out, *wham!* Like a bullet! One of the nurses reacted quickly, dived down and scooped Bird up before she hit the floor. That's why we nicknamed her 'Bird.' "

Bill: "I think you already told me this story."

Sassy lights a cigarette, takes a can of beer out of the refrigerator and goes back to watching TV.

Daybreak, on the Strip in Las Vegas. The neon signs are blinking. On the deserted sidewalk an obese transvestite with pale, indistinct features approaches Bird, who's walking in the opposite direction. She stops and watches him pass by. He's got enormous flaccid breasts, wads of fat. His translucent cock and balls swing from side to side as he walks down the silent street.

The Chameleon is going for a stroll to visit the writer. Bird's decided to stay in bed, look out the window and watch the rain. It could last a while.

He feels a twinge of emotion the moment he sets foot in the wooden shack. The writer isn't up yet. His table has been pushed in front of the bay window that looks out onto the ocean. The typewriter sits like a small Roman temple in the midst of ruins of papers and notes. The manuscript is fairly thick. Everything is saturated with the smell of burning wood from the fireplace. "The Egyptians prostituted themselves to crocodiles." Sade. That's the writer's last line in his open notebook.

The writer stumbles into the kitchen to make some coffee. Meanwhile, the Chameleon takes a peek in the bedroom. The two windows facing the ocean are both open. The black blanket is still there, along with the wrinkled pillowcase. The clothes are still on the floor.

The room next door is devoted to souvenirs of Bird. Letters, photos, cotton from Mississippi, cassettes and a tape recorder, fragments of a life, true stories, dreams, inventions, and various objects. It's a miniature depot for recycled scrap, a compacter of reveries.

The writer pisses in the sink, goes out on the terrace with

his coffee, a mango, and a piece of cake. Burying his feet in the sand, he contemplates the chapter he's about to write. He traces the letters A-L-O-N-E with his forefinger, then erases them. He still has a good hour to savor the juicy bits of mango, dripping all over his hand. He's taken on some color since he's been living at the beach. He hasn't shaved for at least a week now.

The writer is sitting at the typewriter. He begins a sentence that leads to another.

He stops working around seven o'clock, slips on some jeans, and goes for a stroll on the beach. He passes a woman who's walking her dog.

He makes a fire, pours himself a tall glass of bourbon, and rereads his chapter, shouting it out loud. "Not bad," he says before he tosses it into the flames. Once he's sipped half his drink and warms up a bit, he begins all over again.

In the middle of the chapter, he starts to chant: "Alligators . . . Alligators . . ."

The phone rings.

"It's June. I'm having trouble with my dissertation topic. I'd like to talk it over with you."

"Come over in an hour, and bring a bottle of wine and a pizza with mushrooms, peppers, onions and sausage."

"I don't like pork."

"Spice up your life with pork."

"What did you say?"

"Nothing, it's from a commercial. See you later."

June is wearing a oversized turquoise sweatshirt that shows

off her long blue legs. A true blonde, milkfed and full of vita-mins; a picture of hygiene and good health. A delicious pastry for intellectuals, the Chameleon thinks to himself. The girl is all excited to be eating in front of the fireplace with the writer. He passes her the bottle of wine. He notices that she's put on makeup and lip gloss.

"I'd like to do my dissertation on the role of sodomy in *The Philosophy of the Boudoir*. Is that possible?"

"Why not?"

"Well, I was wondering whether the other professors have access to our dissertations. I'd like this text to remain between the two of us."

"No one else will see it."

"Thank you. I don't how to tell you this . . . I have a problem . . . a problem with sodomy . . . I'm interested in it intellectually, but I've never tried it . . . I'm very attracted to the idea, but my boyfriend refuses to do it."

The writer polishes off the rest of his pizza, a pensive look on his face.

"He tried it once, but I think he was too nervous, too tense, he couldn't do it. Then he got upset and, of course, now he doesn't want to hear about it."

She squirms into another position. The writer holds out the magnum of Lambrusco, and June seizes it with both hands. As she's taking a drink, the writer starts to caress her breasts. She abruptly lowers the bottle.

"What a strange idea, touching a woman's breasts like that!"

"You don't like it?"

"You should kiss me first."

"Oh . . ."

"Europeans are strange. An American would never do a thing like that."

"How many times do you have to fuck by the divine path before you can get to sodomy?"

"At least a few times."

"Have you ever seen any Italian films?"

"I don't think so."

"Go see some Italian films."

"I'd like to have a sexual encounter with you."

"A sexual encounter . . ."

"That's what it's called."

The writer gets up. He takes the keys to his Dodge.

"C'mon. We're going for a ride."

"You want to do it in the car?"

"We have a dialectical problem. We're going to find a translator."

For once, the writer is able to find the Indian before the sun comes up. They dance a while, then they all go back to the trailer.

"June wants to have a sexual encounter. I'm afraid I don't have the access code. She'd also like to experience sodomy."

The Indian lights a candle and puts on some rock music.

"Europeans are animals."

"I know. He wanted to feel my breasts."

The writer decides to go for a swim despite the cold. When he returns, the Indian is in the process of licking June's anus.

"He's fantastic, I've already had two orgasms."

The Chameleon takes advantage of the situation and finishes the pulque. Then he goes to take a nap in the Dodge while the writer drives over to the hangar, puffing on the joint the Indian gave him.

ird hears strange cries. She can't tell whether they're from suffering or joy. She walks through a path full of brambles growing between the trees until she's stopped by a high fence topped with barbed wire. She continues her walk along the barbed-wire fence in the direction of the cries, which sound like muffled barking.

Behind a cluster of trees, she discovers a tennis court where two men are playing in a bizarre fashion. Their step is unsteady. They're only using one ball, and spend the entire time looking for it. Occasionally, they swing their rackets into the empty air. The two men, dressed in some kind of pajama bottoms, with bare chests and bare sunburned feet, come toward the fence. One of them picks up the ball and succeeds in hitting it through the chicken wire. Bird accepts the present and stuffs it into the pocket of her jeans. The two men return to the court, where they remain, silent and exhausted.

"Are you hungry?" the Indian asked.

He brought me to a cheap restaurant with only three tables in the black part of town. They served us some sort of meat loaf glazed with honey and pepper on a piece of wax paper, along with a carton of potato salad and the bottle of bourbon that the Indian was carrying around in his pocket. We were the only customers. The Indian and I couldn't take our eyes off the faces of the two cooks, who were an old couple. They had the sad and feverish gaze of fallen descendants of Africa, yet the smile on their lips, the only generous feature of their bodies, came from faraway places. You could hear African music in the background.

"They have rhythm, music. That's how come they're still around. We don't have anything. Just the desert, silence. Patience, perhaps. One day . . ."

The Indian breaks off and pulls a few worn sheets of stationery from the pocket of his leather pants.

"She was fifteen when she wrote this. It's the beginning of her autobiography. I always keep it with me. You can read it if you want."

I recognized Bird's handwriting. The letters were bigger and rounder:

I have no future. My past is full of loneliness, suffering and emptiness. Eighty percent of my fathers were alcoholics, brutes, or just poor slobs. They came and went like rainbows, looking for more affection than they could ever give. My mother is thirty-six. She works in a bread factory that's called "Rainbo," like an unfinished rainbow. My mother is as white as a slice of bread, absentminded, alcoholic, depressed. Her mind has been sucked out by her vacuum cleaner and our TV, which can only get two colors: pink and blue. The tube is shot. It's obvious, but nobody seems to realize it. Anyway, who would pay for the repair? I want my life to be like a house on fire. No attachments to furniture, photographs, souvenirs, a flea-infested carpet, or the refrigerator and its plastic food.

I'm desperate. I'm not a desperate adolescent, I'm a desperate woman.

It's finally over, this goddamn phase of feeling blue all the time. Now it's a real live emotion, unassailable, like an embryo that's been forming inside me. Sometimes I wish I could abort this suffering. I'm ready to pay the price.

I love being on the road. I know I'll be leaving here soon. I want to experience everything and most of all, write, write, write. I'm afraid of nothing but myself and my loneliness. I'll never allow myself to get stuck in a city, a house, a love affair. I want freedom. America is a big country. I love books. I love to hitchhike. I want to find out everything there is to know about people, but I'm afraid to ask them. To fill this emptiness, I answer all the questions. Not personal questions, just the ones you find in magazines. I hold on to to all the questionnaires and I jot down the answers. That way, I'm forced to write. I have certain recurrent dreams and I talk to them like you would friends. I love music, I love jazz. Books are sacred. They're a part of me. Everything I've ever seen, heard or felt is all a part of me. I never feel like there's a past or a future. Everything's in the present. Everything is alive and recorded inside me. Life is like a highway. I love speed, landscapes, accidents. Sometimes I feel like living, other times I feel like dying. I don't believe in love. Writing is like shooting up. A fleeting rush of pleasure. I don't give a shit about wounding myself. Here I am, alive. I want to write the way Charlie Parker played sax. For the sake of music.

I take off my clothes and look at myself in the bathroom mirror. My feet are long and narrow, like in a painting I once saw: a corpse lying on a table in an amphitheater. My skin is pale because I love the night. I'm petite, my body is hard, but my skin is soft. I have fairly long legs, like an animal who's ready for flight, I know that I'm attractive, but I'm not sure if I'm beautiful. I had asthma when I was little and I did a lot of gymnastics. My breasts are small and conical like Chinese straw hats. My shoulders are rounded, my back is muscular and triangular from swimming. My hands are small and my fingers are short, as if they came from one of my fathers and my feet from another. I'm sure that's what happened. My mother never knew how to say "no" to a guy.

Now my face: I have circles around my eyes, my skin is as pale as the rest of my body. I have almond-shaped eyes—the classic literary description, but I really do. My eyes are a very dark brown, almost black. I often wrinkle my forehead. The only thing that attracts me about growing old is having wrinkles. I do everything possible to get them as soon as I can. I hardly sleep. I don't try to avoid pain. My hair is thick and black, long and straight. But one of these days, I'm going to cut it very short. I have a small nose that's a little bit flat, and a very pretty groove between my nose and my mouth. My teeth are spaced in a funny way. I don't know what that's from. I look like some kind of animal when I laugh.

A picture postcard of Eric Dolphy, sent from Seattle:

> Jazz may come from the French word *jaser,* or from black slang, where the word means "to fuck." As early as the eighteenth century, in the South, the French allowed the slaves to bury their dead to the sound of the few instruments they were permitted to have in their possession.
>
> Bird

She's hungry. Her legs are hurting her. She's floating around the streets, surrounded by skyscrapers. She goes into a McDonald's. She finishes off someone's leftover French fries and two bites of hamburger swimming in ketchup. At first, she notices only the dark and feverish eyes with deep circles around them. Then the teeth of a carnivore and the lips, almost white.

"Would you like some dessert?"

"A hamburger, an apple turnover and a coffee."

He goes over to order. Bird takes a sip of his Coke. He looks like either a painter, a writer, or a bum.

He lets her eat in peace. He watches her.

"Anger . . . Lots of anger . . ."

She stares back at him, her face partially hidden behind the white cup. If the coffee weren't so hot, she'd have thrown it in his face.

"Do you need some money?"

"Are you willing to give me some or are you trying to buy yourself a piece of meat?"

"I want to buy you for your music."

"I don't play the flute and I sing badly. Screaming is what I do best."

"I like screaming."

"How much will you give me?"

"How much do you want?"

"Three hundred dollars in advance."

"I must have about eighty dollars on me. I'll give you the rest tomorrow."

"OK."

"But you have to stay with me for twenty-four hours."

"Three days if you want, I couldn't care less, but if you don't pay up, you'll never forget it."

"I'll never forget it anyway. I'm going to turn your body into a symphony."

"I don't like metaphors. You want to get laid? You'll get laid. And a good lay, too."

"I've got stuff to eat at my studio. Shall we go?"

Canal Street. The smell of guava, of ginger. A deadbolt door with three locks leads into a basement that's been converted into a recording studio. There are microphones, wires, a mixing board, tape recorders, and shelves lined with tapes.

"So we're really talking about music, huh?"

The composer makes some coffee. They sit down on a long sofa of purple velvet that looks like it was carted in off the street. The studio is harshly lit. There's a sink, a refrigerator, and a microwave oven. A cot in a corner.

"You live here?"

"I have a room not too far from here, but I sleep here sometimes."

"I like this light."

"Take off your clothes. I'll put on the heat. I've been thinking about doing this for months and when I saw you before, I knew right away that I'd do it with you."

"What do you mean?"

"I'm going to stick mikes all over the place. I'm going to record all of the music your body makes."

While he's talking, the composer shows her the mikes he has in every size. He unwinds the cables.

"I think you'd be more comfortable if you'd lie down on the sofa."

"You don't really think that you're going to stick a mike up my cunt, do you?"

"You can skip it and still keep the eighty dollars."

"Actually, I find this interesting."

"Do you think you can swallow this tiny little mike?"

"I'll try. I won't get electrocuted?"

"No."

"And once you've stuffed me with all these things, then what am I supposed to do?"

"Anything that'll make noise."

"Go buy some condoms. I'll slip the mikes in myself."

"I knew you'd do it."

"If they can record the sounds that a whale makes, why not record the way I sound too?"

"The hardest part will be swallowing the microphone."

"Maybe you could buy some cough syrup with an anesthetic in it."

Bird gets undressed, covers herself up and falls asleep on the sofa. She doesn't hear the composer when he comes in. He pours himself a glass of Chablis and observes Bird's expression, peaceful in the light. Suddenly, he has an idea. He'll call this new work *Inner Life*.

Bird is naked, wires are coming out of every orifice of her body. A headset lets her hear the incredible mix of sounds coming from her insides. She's overwhelmed by a kind of euphoria, she starts to improvise, create new sounds by varying the rhythm of her breathing, contracting her muscles, undulating her body and stroking herself with the microphone that she puts up her vagina. Her moans reverberate with an entirely different depth than the ear would normally perceive. She sings, she cries, she murmurs, she talks, she whistles, she uses her belly like the skin of a drum, she swallows some food, drinks a glass of wine. She gets up and takes a step, listening to the hissing, the whistling, to the infinite range of vibrations created by her body. She ends up dancing to the sound of her own music until she exhausts herself completely. Her dripping body sinks into a blue trance, into a senseless oblivion.

The Chameleon follows the gray outline of the writer. The farther along he gets with his book, the more he fades into the muted colors of dawn. Despite the cold, the writer is only wearing a cotton shirt, a lightweight pair of pants and espadrilles. His eyes are wide open, his body seems to have shrunk. The recollection of the night he has just spent with the girl has already evaporated, like the hot fleeting aroma of the rum they'd consumed. The Chameleon had to satisfy himself with the last few drops in the bottle. The evening had been as insipid as something out of *Modern Romance*. The writer fell asleep almost immediately afterward; the girl made a long phone call to one of her friends to tell her all about the ineptitude of the writer as a young dog, and then took a Valium to make her sleep. She'd left the light on. The Chameleon observed their bodies, lying there unaware of each other even in their sleep. The girl slept with her mouth open. The Chameleon couldn't resist slipping his forefinger inside and letting it wander around her teeth and palate. The writer slept on his back, his left leg touching the floor and his face agitated by nervous tics.

The Chameleon made do with the only book he could dig up in the house: *Cajun Cooking*. After reading about twelve different recipes, he had eaten some fruit and dozed off in an armchair.

The writer slides out of bed. He picks up his clothes and gets dressed on his way out. Now he's walking into the gray morning, looking for his car. He stops in front of a warehouse. A rat crosses the street and fixes its beady little eyes on the Chameleon for a moment, who picks up a rock and throws it. The writer bends over, straightens back up and takes a deep breath. He looks pale. He takes a couple of hesitant steps before vomiting up his characters.

Bird is taking a shower, her body racked by violent sobs.

The existence of volcanic activity on the moon is equally suggested by a gigantic fissure on the moon's surface, called the Fault of Hyginus. This fissure is about three kilometers wide and 150 long. An aerial photo reveals a series of craters spread out along the length of the interior of the fault. These craters cannot be due to meteorites, because those would have produced a random distribution of the craters over the whole area. The craters in the Fault of Hyginus must be volcanic, and it is possible that the entire fault is the surface manifestation of a rupture effected from the depths of the lunar body.

The Chameleon can't stop thinking about the isles of mangroves along the vast stretch of the Mississippi. He hangs around Moscow, idling between the liquor store and the room in which Bird is living with a black woman. Moscow, London, Paris: a little triangle that touches the river.

It's a miserable little town surrounded by cotton fields. Bird has been reading Shakespeare for the last two weeks. In the evening, she goes out, wanders from one wooden shack to the next and talks to the people. She's struck up a friendship with a stooped old man who spends all his time sitting on a bench in front of his home, watching the river. Bird listens. He tells her about Moscow:

"Here's what they say: there's the Soviet Union and the complete opposite, America, home of the free. Well, I've been living in Moscow for seventy-eight years now and I know what I'm talking about. You know, all those ideas like: if you're qualified for a job, then you'll get it; if you work hard, you'll be compensated; women are free, blacks are free, you're free to think, create, say whatever you want. You live in a free country and here we don't throw people in jail just for their ideas. You're the master of your own destiny, you pilot your own plane, all you have to do is make loops in the sky and it'll be worth something, it'll be recognized, here you can make a fortune.

That's all bullshit. Responsibility, mastering things, taking matters in hand, all that crap that they hammer us over the head with . . . Where was I?"

"All that crap that they hammer us over the head with . . ."

"They keep telling people that they're free. You're free! You're free! And those people are happy to be free. They follow like sheep . . . C'mon! There you go! Into the mold! Everything that's sticking out gets lopped off. It's the exact same thing for the whites, the Apaches, and the blacks. It's when you try to use your freedom that you realize it's like an old shed snakeskin. Fragile. You can't use a dead skin. The only freedom you're given is the one to conform. We live in a country of freedom. Me, I watch the river. Nobody has to tell it that it's free, but when it overflows, it floods our homes, it changes color without warning, it's uncontrollable. Now that's freedom. Over there, in the other Moscow, they tell you: you're free to serve the government, which means the people. You're free to obey. So everyone revolts, to survive. They pay the price. But in our country, they tell you that everything's free. A free gift, like they say on TV. Free gift! People have got to understand that freedom isn't like a bar of gold that you can bury in your garden, and think that you're rich. It's got to be spent. That's the only way you find out whether you have it or you don't. This Moscow is just like that other Moscow. Only here, it's even harder to get yourself out of a mess. We're all hypnotized by words.

I'm glad that you came to watch the river with me. Will you come back tomorrow?"

"I'll be staying for a few more days."

"There's some fresh cornbread in the kitchen. Go get some so we can taste it."

"It's good. Do you want some more?"

"My mother used to make it that way. It's good when it's warm. When you can smell and taste it at the same time."

"Tomorrow I'll bring along some dinner."

"When I'm about to die, I want to be sitting on a log so I can float down the river all the way to the ocean, like an old black sailor."

Bird is coming out of a forest. She crosses a wheatfield. A fringe of clouds unravels in the amethyst sky.

Bird goes past a place where the wheat has been flattened out. She stops there, lies down, watches the sky.

Bird: Clouds, moon, sun, shooting stars, rockets, cosmic dust, fragments of disintegrated planets, airplanes, flies, atomic mushrooms, hailstones, rain, snow, butterflies, birds, bodies, moon rocks, asteroids, mirages, divinities, dung, lightning, thunder, piss, spit, missiles, dreams, hats (she throws hers), glasses, T-shirt, shoes, socks, jeans, panties (she throws each object after having taken it off).

Bird starts to run through the wheat, continuing her list and shouting each word: parachutes, palm trees, houses, cars, Bird, stop, bridges, tornadoes, emptiness, blue, red, gray, sulfur yellow, malachite, brown, fruit, acorns, chestnuts, bird semen, airplane fuel, pollution, pollen, leaves, flowers, mosquitoes, songs, diamond shapes, music, cries, the rustling of wheat, liquid color, flags, flying men, heads of giraffes, cosmonauts, satellites, bottles, paper airplanes, suicides, thoughts.

Breathless, Bird stumbles onto a road that runs alongside the field. Standing with her legs slightly apart, she pisses on the asphalt.

Solitude. I opened the yellow paper envelope. I found twenty-four black-and-white photos, with no other message.

A subway station. Twelve somewhat blurry profiles, among which I recognize Bird's. She's wearing her jeans and her leather jacket, her hair is swept upward by the rush of air from the passing subway car. Out of all these ghostly silhouettes, only Bird's emerges, her body like a tightly strung bow, her gaze distant. Her pale profile stands out against the dark background. Her shoulders are slightly hunched from the way her hands are thrust into the pockets of her jacket. Force. Emotion.

An unmade bed. There's a carcass of half a chicken on a paper plate, the bones broken off and cleaned; a white towel with which X wiped his hands after eating. A spotlight next to the bed illuminates the scene. The rest of the room is dark. The white sheet reflects the light. The corner of a book sticking out from under the pillow. Bird's scent emanates from this photo. I can smell her.

A portrait of Bird, from the neck up. She's changed since the beginning of her trip. The hastily cut hair frames her face, set in a deliberately immobile expression, with no trace of a smile or any tension. Something white. Everything is concentrated in her gaze, staring into the lens of the camera. This look goes right through me as no other look ever has. The photo is burning my hand.

A motel signboard, at night. The green neon light outlines the silhouette of a palm tree. A cascade of yellow stars and the letters "STARDUST" in red. That's how I imagine it.

Her right arm is cut off by the frame just before the place where it meets her shoulder; the elbow is bent, the hand open, soft and sensual; the short fingers, artlessly curled. There's a certain roundness to the forearm, a speck of shadow on the elbow, and the entire biceps muscle is lightly contoured. Bird appears to be stretched out on a piece of light-gray paper, the kind used by photographers. The lighting is very soft, probably filtered.

The next photo is one of her left arm outstretched, with her palm pressed against the paper. My eyes linger on the shape of her wrist, move along the length of her tendons, just visible beneath the skin, and proceed all the way down to her short, square little fingernails.

A straight road disappears into the horizon. The photo was taken from the inside of a car, with the hood in the foreground. From the looks of the hubcap, it's probably a Dodge.

.   .   .

I went to get a pair of scissors to cut up the photos, to rearrange them at the places where her limbs join together, and then start to reassemble Bird's body by tacking up the fragments on a white wall.

The next photo framed the base of her neck, her rounded shoulders, her shoulder joints and dark, somewhat hairy armpits, her chest and her small, conical breasts. A compact and slightly angular body.

I decided to finish reassembling this body before looking at the other photos. The navel, the hips and the pelvis had appeared in the preceding photo, but taken from a slightly different position. This prevented the lines from joining perfectly and added certain angles to the contours of the body that made it look more like an abstract image. Her navel plunged inward. The thighs and the legs were added in two remaining photographs, completing this nearly life-size nude.

I picked up all the other pictures and hung them in a circle around Bird's body, but at a distance, as if to keep their separate stories out of the way.

A smashed-up car that does not look like a Dodge.

The picture of a steer hooked on a rack inside a truck.

.   .   .

A tenor saxophone lying in an open case.

The pale and washed-out stare of an old man.

A young girl crying in a phone booth.

The moon, a tiny spot in the center of darkness.

Icy pleasure.

A police car pulls up in front of Sassy's bungalow. Flanked by two cops, Bird gets out, wearing only a scrap of oilcloth.

The officers knock. Bird's father answers the door.

A policeman: "We found her downtown, she was walking around completely naked. You should pay more attention to what your daughter is doing."

The father: "There's no end to it. Come look in her room. It's not as though she doesn't have any clothes, but as soon as it starts to get hot, she leaves the house, takes off her clothes wherever she is and goes on for miles like that."

The other policeman: "You better watch her more closely."

The policemen reclaim their square of oilcloth and leave. Bird remains where she is. The father paces the living room. He kicks the television and it topples off its stand. Bird screams. Her father picks her up and throws her out the window.

There was nothing but a color chart inside the envelope: colored cardboard rectangles on a string, like the kind sold in art-supply shops. I examined them one by one, hoping to find a message. The only thing that caught my eye was that some of the rectangles were rippled or that others were faded. The fan of colored shapes sat on top of my work table. I liked looking at it.

The next day, while at my desk, I accidentally dropped my notepad. When I bent down to pick it up, my face was about an inch away from the range of colors. My senses were instantaneously aroused. The cardboard was giving off a smell. At first I thought it was coming from just one of the pieces. I figured that Bird must have kept the color chart close to her body—I recognized the distant scent of her skin—but after having sniffed each rectangle, I realized that each one had a different smell. I was fascinated: it was impossible to identify them with any precision. It was only through observing the relationship between the colors and the smells that my thoughts became clearer. Later on, I placed each piece of cardboard on my tongue, where it softened and penetrated my senses. I reconstructed a body with blots of color that were strangely obscure. Only the shade of blue left no doubt in my mind. It was a fixed center, blinking on and off with unnerving power.

B ehind the wheel of a red Impala convertible, Bird is riding down a path surrounded by tropical vegetation. The branches whip the sides of the car, until the jungle seems to close in on itself above her. There are no other tracks on this dirt road; it is as if Bird were the first to have ever used it.

Bird stops the car, takes out a big bottle of Jack Daniel's and continues on foot. The path turns into a trail. Jungle music.

Once she's gone past the edge of the forest, Bird discovers a sand creek and a bamboo house built on pilings that one reaches by means of a bridge. The sun has just gone down. Bird enters, ventures down a hallway with several rooms giving off it on either side, and ends up in a kitchen. There's an old black woman fanning the embers as she kneels over a clay hearth where a pot of gumbo is simmering. Her movements are slow, harmonious. She's wearing nothing but a loincloth made of some red material. Her breasts and skin, furrowed with deep wrinkles, her legs, which are still muscular, and her calm face are illuminated by the fading twilight.

Mia: "Welcome."

Bird: "Were you expecting me?"

Mia: "The seashells say many things."

Bird: "Is Oswald still alive?"

Mia: "Come, he's in his hammock. He hardly ever leaves it these days."

Bird: "I brought him some bourbon."

Mia: "He'll like that. He has very few visitors and we never go out."

Bird: "Are you his wife?"

Mia: "I was his nurse. As you can see, I don't have nipples anymore, he ate them off. Then, it must have been when he was around ten, he gave me a daughter who became his wife, Zoe. They had a daughter, Jasmine. Then it was her turn to be taken by Oswald. She had Harmonia, who gave birth to our youngest girl, Boto, who's about fifteen. When he can get out of his hammock, Oswald sometimes tries to make her pregnant, but I doubt if he can still do it."

Bird: "No boys?"

Mia: "We ate them all. When Oswald dies, we'll look for another man."

Mia and Bird come to a large terrace where old Oswald is letting himself be rocked by the evening breeze. Mia pulls up a bamboo chair and touches Oswald's shoulder. He's a tall, thin old man, weathered by the sun. He opens his eyes, runs his fingers through his white hair and smiles.

Oswald: "She looks a lot like the visitor we've been expecting. . . . We're happy to have you here."

Bird holds out the bottle to him. He unscrews it, takes a swig, then passes it to Mia and Bird who also take a drink.

Oswald: "One of the rare gifts of civilization. You'll stay with us for a few days, won't you? You can share Boto's hammock—she's the slightest of my female companions. Ah, speak of the devil, here she is."

Boto is just coming out of the water with a fish skewered on her bamboo harpoon, naked, her black skin dripping wet, her head spiked with tiny braids. Laughing, she runs up to the terrace. She throws the fish on Oswald's stomach.

Boto: "Here, this one's still moving."

When her turn comes, she takes a sip of bourbon, which she immediately spits out.

Boto: "We were all waiting for you. It's so rare that we have visitors."

Oswald: "In the beginning there were FBI agents, a few journalists, and some who were just curious. The publication of my *Cannibal Manifesto* in 1928 shocked certain intellectuals. I had to go into exile, settle down in this deserted place."

Bird: "I've heard of it, but I've never read it."

Oswald: "The only remaining copies were destroyed. It's a collector's item. No one has ever been able to publish it again. The White House was afraid that students might become enthusiastic and put my principles into practice. A cannibalistic nation isn't possible in these times, but perhaps you and Boto will see its advent."

Bird: "Do you have a copy?"

Oswald: "No, we know it by heart. It's the only culture we have."

Boto runs her fingers through Bird's hair.

Boto: "Come and play in the ocean. Afterward, we'll eat fish, fried bananas and fruit, then we'll go sleep in my hammock. I'll recite Oswald's *Manifesto* for you."

Bird: "Where are Zoe, Jasmine and Harmonia?"

Oswald takes a few more swigs of bourbon.

Mia: "We each have our own job. I cook, Boto fishes, Zoe farms the grain, Harmonia cuts and bundles it, Oswald hunts. But these days we eat mostly fish because Oswald hasn't brought back any wild pigs or birds or snakes."

Mia picks up the fish that is pressed against Oswald's side. Bird undresses; Boto pinches her white skin, touches her pubic hair and laughs.

They dive into the red ocean, playing together like dolphins.

It's nighttime. Oswald, Mia, Zoe, Jasmine, Harmonia, Boto and Bird are sitting under the veranda, grouped around various dishes served on banana leaves. They're eating with their fingers. Boto makes compact little balls that she rolls between her fingers before sliding them into Bird's mouth. An oil lamp lights their faces and their bodies.

The breeze blows through the bamboo slats. Boto and Bird are lying in a hammock. You can hear the jungle and its night sounds: cries, bird songs, murmurs.

Their bodies seem glued to the air. Intertwined, they sparkle, caressing each other. Boto speaks very softly into Bird's ear.

Boto: "Cannibalism, alone, unites us. Socially. Economi-
cally. Philosophically. Cannibalism is the only law in the world.
It's the hidden expression of every individualist."

Boto kisses Bird's shoulder.

Boto: "We're against all forms of catechism. The only
thing that interests me is what's not mine. That's the law of
man, the law of the cannibal. There's no more mystery woman
or built-in psychology. The truth is hindered by the clothes men
wear, the imperviousness that comes between the inner and
outer world. We revolt against the clothed man."

Boto nibbles Bird's belly.

Boto: "We don't write with the body. No canned consciousness. No original sin. We live according to the rights of
the somnambulist. We've swallowed up the conceptions of the
world. There's no such thing as logic. There's no difference
between mind and body. We live in the oral world. Justice from
the outside world is only a code for vengeance, and science, a
code for magic."

Boto puts Bird's fingers in her mouth and nibbles them.

Boto: "We're against the irreversible world and embalmed
ideas. Against systems that diminish our inner conquests. Instinct is cannibalistic knowledge joined with the sky and the
earth. I'll eat the one who provides me with the answers. The
Truth is simply the Lie repeated over and over again. We know
the riddles. The creation of Morality is actually the true igno-

rance of things, the lack of imagination, the repression of infantile curiosity. Civilization produces a debased man. We eat the civilized in order to give them access into the lack of culture."

Boto sucks on Bird's breast, stroking her face. Then she falls asleep on her chest.

Night. Embers on the beach. Mia, Jasmine, Zoe, Harmonia and Boto have each painted their bodies with a white stripe that runs from the forehead down to the pelvis. Bird wears the same line, but in black. The six women are lying in the sand; their bodies, contorted during the trance, are now gradually relaxing. Mia is the first to rise. She gathers together several bones. The other women join her. Each of them emits a soft and plaintive tone with no variation of pitch, that fades as they exhale.

Mia returns to the bungalow and comes back with Oswald's hammock. She gives it to Bird.

Bird is twelve years old. At dusk, she climbs out of her bedroom window. She takes off her pajamas, scales a tree and jumps. She rolls onto the ground, picks herself up, climbs higher, jumps. A third time, from an even greater height, she throws herself into the deep blue.

"Something Like a Bird," Mingus's last album. Confined to a wheelchair, he could neither play nor lead the musicians, but his presence in the studio was enough to fill the music with all the raging ferocity of his soul.

Bird slips the cassette into her Walkwoman. The subway glides along in the dark as she dances. A merciless dance. A shining steel rail.

Bird goes into a bookstore. She pages through a collection of poems by William Carlos Williams:

This Is Just to Say

I have eaten
the plums
that were in
the icebox

and which
you were probably
saving
for breakfast

Forgive me
they were delicious
so sweet
and so cold

Later, she found a poem by Tabito:

The plum-tree planted by my wife
Whene'er I look upon,
My heart is choked with sorrow,
And my tears flow down.

Bird goes into a movie theater.

"Taxi! Are you free?"

"Go fuck yourself!"

"I'm in a big hurry . . ."

"So wait your turn, like everybody else."

"The Wilshire."

"You don't know anything about music, do you?"

"Drive faster."

"Haydn was a genius who hasn't really been discovered yet. He served as Beethoven's wet nurse and . . ."

"What route are you taking?"

"I should never have let you into my concert hall."

"Do you have a cigarette?"

"You're afraid . . . I can feel it."

"Afraid of what? Of your music?"

"Afraid of getting killed by the four guys in the limousine who've been following us ever since you got in. You took me for a jerk. I don't like it when people take me for a jerk. I'm not a jerk."

"I don't understand how a guy like you can play Haydn."

"The sensitivity of the soul has nothing to do with the outer appearance."

"Do you remember the name of the hotel?"

"What hotel? What's your name?"

"Laura. What's yours?"

"Haydn . . . That's what they call me."

"Joseph?"

"So you do know something about music . . ."

The frozen grass crunches under Bird's feet. A shower of sparks shoots out into the night. The trees are losing their orange and blue leaves. Violet birds with white wings soar against the backdrop of the black sky. She stops to buy a hot dog and continues down Seventh Avenue.

Bird goes into a movie theater.

"I came all the way down here to see if Terry was around."

"She's probably watching TV."

"How much more do you have left?"

"Of what?"

"How much more do you have left?"

"What are you talking about?"

"Just tell me how much more you have left!"

"Two . . . I think . . ."

"OK, give me one."

"Here. It's good stuff."

"I don't understand why you lie all the time . . ."

"I don't lie."

"Yes you do, you never quit."

"I've had about enough . . ."

"Look, I called three times, I asked you if Terry was there, you said yes, I come all the way across town and Terry isn't here . . ."

"She was watching TV a little while ago. I saw her . . ."

"What was she watching?"

"Something stupid, a movie, a thing about ants, why they run around all over the place, what they think about and everything, the guy was telling it in a serious voice . . . This guy was so serious it was funny. . . . Terry was laughing her head off and so was I. . . . We had a can of beer. . . . There was blood on her sheets. . . ."

"Blood!"

"I think. . . . Or maybe it was ketchup from the other night, when Tom came over with a mountain of French fries and those little packets of ketchup. We might have stepped on one and it could have ripped open and . . ."

"Why didn't you tell me she'd already left when I got here?"

"I thought she was still watching the ants . . ."

"There weren't any shady deals going on here?"

"Ants are always clean. At least they look clean . . ."

"I mean like some junky who might have dropped over to pick up his fix."

"Go check out the sheets. I think it's ketchup. If Terry got her throat slit, she'd still be in front of the TV. No one would be able to get her out of here without me seeing it. You owe me twenty dollars."

"You can shove it. I came here to see Terry, I came all the way across town . . ."

"But she was here. Anyway, I saw her."

"That doesn't mean a thing."

"Take your dirty hands off me, don't touch me! You're nuts!"

"Yeah."

"You make me sick."

"You're nuts too."

"I felt like seeing you, Superman."

"Me too. That's why I told you Terry was here."

"What are you looking at?"

"Your ass."

"I can tell that you're looking at my ass."

"I like it a lot."

"OK, I'm getting out of here."

"Wait a second. Terry went out to get some nail polish."

"She's going to paint her nails?"

"Yeah, I asked her to."

"What color?"

"Some kind of red."

"Really?"

"Don't you ever wear any?"

"It depends."

"It reminds me of cherries. Sometimes she scratches me."

"You enjoy it?"

"Yeah, it feels good."

"OK, I'm getting out of here."

"That's her. I just heard her come in."

"Joy, how long have you been here?"

"This asshole scared me with the sheets."

"He always wants to screw me when I have my period."

"Frankly, I don't give a fuck."

"It reminds me of cherries."

"If you say so."

"OK, well I'm still gonna split."

"You don't want to watch *Lady Blue*? We can order out for some Chinese food and watch TV."

"I've gotta be somewhere at midnight."

"What would you rather have, beef, chicken or pork?"

"The stuff with the noodles."

"OK. Hello. Shao Lin Temple, this is Terry. I'd like a chicken with almonds, an onion beef, an order of rice and a chow mein."

"It's Colombian."

"If I hadn't come across town, I would never have gotten any of it."

"You have a sixth sense. I told Ron that you'd be coming over."

"Do you think ants get stoned?"

"Yeah. One day I saw one lying on its back."

"Maybe it was sunbathing."

"Sunbathing? An ant?"

"That guy was saying how civilized they were."

"Who's supposed to come over tonight?"

"No one. I've nothing left."

"Terry, will you come and take a shower with me?"

"If you want. It was so hot in the car. And there was that bastard sniffing me."

"He's nice, but he's an animal."

"I'm not an animal, I'm seventy-five percent human."

"I'm going to wash my hair."

"Me too."

"Ron, call us when the food gets here."

"I'll wait for you in bed."

"Put on some music."

"Go powder your pussy."

"Fuck you, Ron."

The Chameleon's face is like a blurry photograph. It leaves a vague impression. Eyes, mouth, nose, ears, hair. He's tall, thin, and wears a gray raincoat and motorcycle boots. You can see his rainbow-colored flesh through the transparent skin. If you get a chance to stare at his face, it's as if there is nothing there but a huge nose and eyes—eyes that you'll later remember at times when your mind is blank, and your body empty. A red iris floating in a crystalline black.

Bird looks over her shoulder and tries to memorize this face. All that remains is a river of paint flowing into the night.

Bird goes into a movie theater.

"Let's find a quiet place to talk."

"Come over to my place."

"No, I'd rather be on neutral ground."

"The bus?"

"That would be perfect."

"I don't know if it was a good idea for you to come back."

"I can't stand being alone."

"I know they just closed the factory. It was in the papers."

"That's not why I came back, Jane."

"Let's say it isn't."

"We can talk it over, start from the beginning, figure it all out."

"We've done that ten times already."

"I'm coming back to live with you."

"I think it's too late. I waited five months for you and all that time, not one postcard, not one phone call, nothing. I didn't even know if you were alive. That's why I can't forgive you. All the rest I can gradually forget."

"You'll forget about that, too."

"I don't think so. Some things don't go away, they come back to haunt me every night."

"I know. I've been through that myself."

"Because of me?"

"No, not because of you."

"I have the feeling we've already finished our inventory."

"You talk like the guys in the factory."

"I can lend you a little money. You can find a cheap hotel."

"I think I need a little time to do nothing, see what happens. I could move into your garage until the fall."

"I know you. You'll always be hanging around the house."

"No. I'll buy myself a hot plate, a TV. I'll only come in if you invite me."

"I just don't want to hear you pacing back and forth."

"OK. Let's forget it. I'll go find a motel. We'll see each other every now and then, like we're doing today."

"Maybe things will change."

"It's been great seeing you. You get more and more beautiful every day."

"Let's go. I start work at six tomorrow."

"I've got an idea . . ."

It had been raining. The sidewalk glistened. A young man is dancing alone in front of the entrance to the subway. In the back seat of a limousine, a black man is having a drink while he watches TV.

"Hey, you!"

Bird stops.

"Come watch the game."

Bird opens the car door and slides in.

"You want something to eat? I'll ask the chauffeur to go out and get some ribs."

"That would be great."

"It looks like there's a giant orange cloud over the city tonight."

"My name is Bird."

"I'm Augusto."

Augusto opens the carton of ribs. He pours hot sauce over

them and serves Bird a glass of bourbon. The chauffeur returns with a pile of paper napkins. They chew and suck the bones, then put them on the lid of the carton.

Through the open window, Bird watches a woman in shorts. Rolls of greenish fat spill out all over. Her charcoal hair waves in the night breeze. Two sky-blue breasts wobble under a creamy pink T-shirt.

"She'd make a magnificent saint . . ."

"Are you a pimp?"

"No, but I used to be. Now I'm in theater. I'm waiting for a friend who's in a show."

Bird goes into a movie theater.

"We're all extraterrestrials."

"I hope that we can at least find a way to give birth in space without the enemy's radar being able to figure out our birth rate."

"The best scientists of Gzaour are working on it every minute. From the reports I've received, it'll be possible to plant embryos in a galactic spaceship, but we need an exceptional security force. We could lose a year's population in a few seconds."

"Houara thinks that we could use a whale as a surrogate mother."

"I think that would be more discreet."

"Let's wait for the coming moons and consult the oracle."

. . .

A man with the trunk of an elephant hands Bird a card as she's walking down Seventh Avenue. She gazes at the neon sign of a peepshow, The Blue Paradise, and decides to go inside. A woman in a zebra skin gives her a pile of tokens. She goes into a private booth and puts a token in the machine. A metal shutter opens immediately. In a palace of mirrors that endlessly reflect the bodies, Bird watches an alligator-man put his gigantic virile member into the navel of a siren with multicolored scales. When the alligator-man comes, he covers the siren with a coat of glaze that fossilizes on the velvet stage.

"For only twenty dollars you can see a special show, don't miss it!"

Day after day, the image of Bird's body darkened when exposed to light, taking on a silver reflection. I was convinced that she'd wanted this transformation to occur and that the pictures had only been partially developed, causing her body to sink into the darkness. As soon as I became conscious of this phenomenon, I brought the photos into a room that I never used and covered the only window with a navy-blue bath towel. This way, I could slow down the inevitable vanishing of the images that I found so fascinating.

I installed a red lightbulb in the ceiling fixture, and every night, after the fire had died out and I'd stayed there a while longer in the silence and the dark, thinking about tomorrow's chapter, I would go into this room and watch the interesting mutation of Bird's body. I was astonished by her beauty, her cruelty, the pleasure she derived from playing this game, her creativity—how she could give more and more of herself, take it to the extreme, scattering a trail of steel tacks behind her, which would gradually melt inside me, then crystallize in my mind. Her body continued to empty itself of its substance and to fill up with night and air. Yet the image that remained was at certain moments strangely incandescent. There were times when I'd wake up with this image in my mind, along with the burning sensation that was so infinitely pleasurable.

. . .

Eventually the picture turned completely black. That day, I brought all the photos back into the living room and sometimes, in the glare of the midday sun, I thought I could make out a form, the crater of her navel or her steely gaze. But, in reality, there was nothing left.

Bird's bare feet standing on glass beads.

One of the surprises of the lunar landing was the result of the examination of the lunar dust under a microscope: a good part of it was made up of small beads of glass. It seems that their existence is due to the impact of meteorites that provokes a fusion of part of the lunar soil, which in the process throws off a fine mist of droplets. Being very small in size—several hundreths of a millimeter in diameter—they cool off quickly, taking the shape of small glazed spheres.

A car pulls up in front of Lincoln Cemetery in Kansas City. Bird gets out, a small bouquet of flowers in her hand. She follows a path into the wooded hills.

Bird stops in front of a sinister-looking red shack. The dogs are barking. She knocks on the glass door. An old man answers.

The guardian: "What do you want?"

Bird: "Where is Charlie Parker's grave?"

The guardian: "Who?"

Bird: "Charlie Parker!"

The guardian: "CHARLES Parker. . . . Go up that path to where it loops around. It's right across from there."

The guardian disappears into the darkness of his shack.

Bird walks past the tombstones set into the grass. She comes to the loop. Black marble, a small patch of grass, a stone border. Bird throws her flowers, which scatter onto the grave. She picks up a pink plastic carnation she finds on the tombstone, and sits down. Tears, wind in the trees, her gaze is lost among the rolling hills.

Voice of a black man: "He wanted to study with Paul Hindemith at Yale. Whenever you'd talk to him about other sax players, he'd say: 'There's lots of room at the top.'"

Voice of a white man: "He always kept a mouthpiece in his

pocket. He could play three times as many notes on his alto as anyone else."

Voice of a black man: "Charlie was interested in the Moslem religion. His name was Saluda Hakim. He loved the cinema, women, waiters and taxi drivers."

A white psychiatrist: "A superior intelligence with paranoid tendencies. A hostile and elusive personality, with primitive drives and sexual fantasies. We diagnosed him as a latent schizophrenic."

A white man: "From the time he was fourteen, he'd spend his nights in the yard behind the clubs where all of the greats were playing: Lester Young, Coleman Hawkins and all the other musicians of that time. That's how he got his nickname, 'Yardbird.' He used to say that his inspiration came from Mecca. He loved Heifetz, Prokofiev, Ravel. He was constantly fucking the girls who hung out in the clubs. There was a strength, a savage force in him. He had an old sax made in Paris in 1898 that was wrapped with adhesive tape—it wasn't really even an instrument. Parker played for two dollars a night, when he showed up. Later on, I bought him a sax for a hundred and ninety dollars. Many years later, he got himself a Selmer. He'd practiced so long on terrible instruments that he could get a sound out of anything. It was Ben Webster who first realized the importance of this kid. It was at Minton's. Ben walked in. He listened and said: 'Where did this crazy guy come from? I feel like I'm in hell.' He got up, ripped the sax out of Bird's hands and told him: 'This instrument isn't supposed to be able

to play that many notes.' The problem getting hold of Bird—
he'd sleep anywhere he could."

Bird is taking a walk down Vine Street, where all the clubs
used to be. There are hardly any left. She stops in front of the
Gem movie theater, closed today.

A black man: "When a girl asked him: 'What are you
thinking about?', he'd answer: 'Fucking.' With him, you got
down to work right away. He was an ogre. He ate like a horse,
fucked like a bull and played like no one else. He'd get stoned
on nutmeg, it was cheap. A tradition among musicians. He
didn't turn up his nose at the other stuff either. At fifteen, he
was already a junkie. Bird isn't dead, he's hiding away somewhere and one of these days he'll turn up with something new
that looks like death.

A black woman: "He died at the age of thirty-five. Sometimes he'd play his horn in Paseo Park at night, until dawn. He
loved it when a girl would come up in front and dance for him,
it got him incredibly excited, musically. He'd start to fuck her
with his music. He loved their gestures, their faces, their bodies.
He'd put his sax under his pillow and sleep on it."

received a postcard: an aerial view of Manhattan.

     I had this dream: A little girl kept repeating: "What country is this?"

     She was circling around a transparent basin carved from ice, which was resting on a pedestal, filled with a salad of pistols, bloody tampons and diced chunks of brains doused with vinegar.

Bird

"I've done nearly all there is to do in my life . . ."

"What do you mean by that?"

"I'll be eighty years old soon. A clairvoyant told me I'd live to be eighty-one. What do you think I'll die of?"

"Old age. Or maybe an accident. You'll be hit by a car while you're drunk. There are a thousand possibilities."

"I know. Two years ago, I was obsessed with the idea and I made a list. I ended up with three hundred and eighty-seven ways of dying. You must think that's dumb, don't you?"

"No. I think about it a lot myself."

"At first, when you helped me get home, I thought you were a junkie. That wasn't on my list. I said to myself: this little bitch is going to help me up the stairs, she's going to lock me in my apartment, put on the radio or the TV, and she's going to torture me until I tell her where I hide my money. I was scared because everything's in the bank. I must have had about ten dollars on me. So I figured, she's going to try and drag it out of me. I'm going to die. It's a strange thing—fear, suspicion. How about you? You weren't scared?"

"Scared of what?"

"I could have been a crazy old coot, a sex maniac . . . there are any number of possibilities."

"Everything interests me. But you can hardly stand on

your own two feet. One kick and you would have collapsed."

"I could have taken you by surprise while you were asleep."

"I've been on the road for almost a year now. I've seen it all. I have a guardian angel. He would have warned me."

"Where is he?"

"There, in the corner of the room."

"I don't feel his presence."

"You can talk to him. He'd enjoy that."

"Do you talk to him too?"

"All the time."

"Does he answer you?"

"No, I think he just laughs."

The Chameleon doesn't like it when people talk about him so openly. He, who is so discreet. It's true that Bird speaks to him often. She sets traps for him when she's certain that he's close by. Especially at night. The other day, she was taking a bath while the old man had gone to sit in the sun on a bench by the ocean. It was an old round bathtub, deep enough for Bird to stretch out in. Without a moment's hesitation, the Chameleon peeled off his clothes and slipped into the water. He had simply forgotten about Archimedes' principle. Bird watched the water level rise. She started to laugh, then got completely hysterical. She called him every name in the book: motherfucker, birdbrain, alligator, nitwit, tropical submarine, strawberry ice cream, rat face, egg roll, metaphor, fatso, member of the CIA, cranky bear, not to mention the rest. This went

on until the water had turned cold, but the Chameleon didn't
dare flinch at the insults. Finally, the old man walked into the
bathroom. He must have figured she'd brought someone up to
the apartment. He came over to the bathtub and ogled Bird a
little, her breasts in particular. Bird was silent. Eventually, the
old man went out again. He already had enough fantasies spinning around in his head to last him for the rest of his life. It
wasn't every day you met a girl who could flash her stuff like
that. She didn't say anything for a few minutes, and then began
to splash me. It was in a nice way. But what followed wasn't
quite as nice. She asked me if I got a hard-on just looking at her.
It was annoying. In fact, ever since then I've had identity problems. I don't know if I'm supposed to talk about myself in the
third person. "The Chameleon was shocked," or more simply:
that little bitch Bird put her finger on it even though it's intan-
gible. Of course I had a hard-on. But we're not going to start
bringing up my sex life, about which I've been quite discreet
until now. I felt like telling her she had nothing to worry about,
since she was taking the pill. And even if she wasn't, there was
a major philosophical problem to deal with: how invisible
semen from an invisible body, secretly deposited into a visible
body (maybe she thought she was dreaming, since I went about
it while she was in a deep sleep) could manifest itself to the point
of uniting with . . . Hmmm, what do they call it? A woman's
sperm . . . no . . . that's not it. . . . There must be a name for
that liquid . . . I'll have to look it up in an encyclopedia.
. . . In any event, once the fusion of those liquids has occurred,

would an embryo begin to develop? And in what form? It could very well give rise to a monster, half of whom would be invisible—the right side of his body, for instance. I could already visualize this creature: only one eye, only one nostril, only one hemisphere (which one would you choose?), a punk hairdo that plummets into a void, a sensitive musical ear—fine, but try dancing on one leg. . . . And the internal organs? You get a liver but no heart or vice versa. Half an anus. I'll let you imagine the consequences of that. Supposedly, one testicle is enough, but as for the member itself, King Dicky of the Dinky Toys, you can imagine it already. . . . Something exotic looking, like a heart of palm, improperly equipped to satisfy/I'd been oblivious. I should have been using condoms. Let's not forget the possibility that besides a half body, vertically, there's also the half, horizontally. A navel, hips and legs. Can only wear pants. Fewer expenses that way. Or, the complete opposite: a torso that ends in a void, with nothing to support it. Can wear a hat, which is no small privilege. Benefits from the tepid pleasures of the mind. Means of transport through special effects. Could be an extra, or maybe even a Hollywood star. A new myth; millions of miniature replicas in supermarkets all over the world. Children will go to sleep with their "half" dolls, the president will talk about him at charity balls, I'll become, or rather my offspring will become, the symbol of all legless cripples, the famous hero of the Vietnam War. The handicapped will be worshiped by all, they'll replace the preachers. They'll pass on the Word, speak in strange and forgotten tongues. Society women will go to plastic surgeons to be cut in half. The only problem will be demographic. But there'll be an advantage in the case of marriage—everyone will be positively certain of getting a half to unite with. What a felicitous development for matrimonial agencies! I can already hear the slogan: "Find your other half, wherever she might be." But all of this could lead to abuse. Afrikaaners hunting down bicolored individuals. There would be scars. Breaking apart and joining back together. That's fine for our dear author, who's all alone and far away, whereas in my case . . . I mean, his, the Chameleon . . .

"In any case, that's not a real job, being a guardian angel."

"You're going to hurt his feelings."

"Still, this whole thing is strange. You saw me in the street. You could have helped me clamber up the stairs . . . at the very most, put me to bed and left. But you've been here for six days now. I'm used to being alone. With you around, everything's different. I've got to get used to making conversation. I can't walk around bare-assed and all that."

"All what?"

"The little things in life."

"Like what?"

"You know exactly what I mean. When you're alone, you can fart to your heart's content."

"I'm like a moth, I'm here to see, to find things out. Just pretend I'm not around. You don't even have to talk to me."

"You understand, since I don't have a fan and it's hot as

hell, I *like* to walk around bare-assed. My mother was very religious. That's why I don't like angels. Will you be leaving soon?"

"Whenever you want."

"It's not because you're broke?"

"No, I have enough to find a motel."

"I'm scared."

"Scared of what?"

"Of being alone, of daily routines, of death."

"What would you like to do before you die?"

"If you tell me there's an angel living here and that you've been transformed into a fairy, I'll gladly take the plunge. I'm sick and tired of playing cards with the same old magpies. Tired of wondering whether heaven is something my mother made up. I haven't been concerned with any of that ever since you've been here. So, you must be a fairy after all."

"Make a wish and you'll see."

"You'll make it come true?"

"Yes."

"So I won't have to go to heaven anymore."

"Where do you want to go?"

"To hell . . . yeah, hell. That would be great."

"And what if that doesn't exist either?"

"That's something I find hard to believe. I have my reasons."

"What exactly do you want?"

"For you to stop paying attention to me. For you to let me

follow my own path. Take your guardian angel, for example. You leave him alone, right?"

"Not always."

"He's the one who follows you around."

"Sometimes he abandons me. Then he catches up with me again."

"This whole thing is really strange. Really strange . . . You know, I never watch TV. Never."

"So what do you use it for?"

"Ask *it*. You wouldn't dare talk to a TV, would you? You need courage for that. A lot of courage. I started about eight or nine years ago. At first, I didn't pay any attention to it. I used it like everyone does, to watch movies, programs, commercials, and the news. Then one day I said to myself, shit, it's been forty years now that I thought I was watching TV when actually it's been watching me. In the past, I used to think that when you pushed the button, that was it. It closes shut just like an eye. Like a pupil, with the little white spot that runs toward the center of the screen and disappears. Afterward, there's a murky glow that gently fades away during the night. So you think it's all over. That's a mistake. People are too accustomed to that kind of thing. All their life, they're constantly saying: 'I want it, I don't want it anymore. I'm turning on the TV, I'm turning off the TV.' I've carefully observed this whole business. It's like the huge convex eye of a dragonfly, reflecting the light. It's the eye of the angel, huh? No gender, not much expression. That's what I like. It just looks at you like that, in a casual way, undemanding. It doesn't weigh you down. Obviously, there's not much to see. Maybe that's why it doesn't show up. From what they say, electronic circuits are fragile. Therefore you should be able to activate them, heat them up, get them to melt, destroy them. And at that moment, death will come."

"It'll come quickly enough."

"After you reach a certain age, you start to wonder if you'll have to go find it and take it by the hand. Maybe if you make no effort to die, you never do. I've been feeling that way for the last three months. I even thought: 'Well, pal, you've been too lazy. You didn't beckon him to come. You didn't talk to him. He's a snob, he walks right past without greeting you, without the slightest signal, you know it's not the right time just then, but after a while they all arrive, take out their pens, well, you know, it's the same story. And I don't feel like playing that game anymore."

"You want to get out of here?"

"The eye knows that aside from buying the paper and two or three things to nibble on and drink, I'm bound to be home. Shit, I want to go out with a bang. No cowardice, no escape. Something sudden and unexpected, here in this room. That's sweet of you, asking me if I want to get out of here. What would we do? Walk around the city. Push the machinery harder and harder until the pump blows. Drop dead in the desert. We might even hear the trumpets of the cavalry while we're being eaten alive by the scorpions. I have no desire to see the face of John Wayne bending over me, in full Technicolor, as he lifts my head to give me something to drink during that final moment. . . . We'll just stay here. . . . I'll put a blindfold over your eyes . . ."

The Chameleon follows the old man into his bedroom. He digs around in a drawer, pulls out a gun, inspects the barrel and slips the bullets in, one by one. Next, he finishes off a fifth of cognac that's lying by the foot of his bed. The Chameleon is in a sweat. Bird doesn't budge from her chair, her eyes still blindfolded. The old man comes closer to her. With a certain expertise, in spite of his shaking, he clasps the gun with both hands. Bird's face is in the line of fire. The Chameleon decides to forget the deontological code of nonintervention and pulls the carpet out from under the old man at the very second the gun goes off. The bullet lodges in the TV. The Chameleon realizes that he's got to be careful that the author's imagination doesn't terminate this story with a blow on the head. According to the doctor in the ambulance, the old man broke his femur.

Bird walked through the city streets. After that, she could allow herself to believe in providence. Freedom.

I t looks as if Bird has decided to spend the day at the beach. Around two o'clock, she gets up from the sandy hollow where she's been lying to go have a tuna fish salad and a glass of milk for lunch. The Chameleon can feel his sunburn. His skin isn't used to these long sunbathing sessions. When Bird goes swimming, he splashes around right alongside her, then goes to dry off in the shade of the lifeguard station.

The sun has gone down. The Chameleon steals a can of Coke from a young couple who are busy kissing. Bird is listening to McCoy Tyner playing "We Will Meet Again" by Bill Evans.

The Chameleon watches Bird's somber expression, which the music blankets with a heavy shellac. Her brow is furrowed, her lips move to every note, her body trembles lightly.

A reaper in a wheat field. Moving along in a straight line, it clears a wide rectangular passage and releases a cloud of dust into the golden light.

From above, the driver surveys the operation and progress of the machine.

A blue smudge appears in front of him, in the middle of the wheat. Keeping the motor running, he stops the reaper, climbs down and approaches it. Bird, wrapped in a blanket, starts to scream at the top of her lungs. The driver takes her in his arms and returns to the machine.

"Goddamn tornados. You've really been flying through space, haven't you . . . ?"

Standing there motionless until the snow has erased her footprints, Bird is listening. Her hair and eyebrows white with flakes, she takes a deep breath, staring off into the endless horizon that's almost as white as the snow. She tries to remember what's been going through her mind, how much time has passed since the very instant she's decided to stop. In the midst of this whiteness, with no tracks or human scent left behind, no road to follow, it's as though she were the last one on earth. Fragile ribbons of snow loosen themselves from the trees and fall unbroken.

WESTERN UNION
13022 HOLLENBERG
BRIDGETON MO 63044 1 AM

1-01536A354 12/19/86 ICS IMBGD SFA
02851 BRIDGETON MO 12-19 0251P CST
BDGC

MR D. WRITER
8431 ARIOLA DRIVE
FICTION CITY KO 76522

PHNMBR
912 678 0002

1-007844A567 12/19/86
ISC IMPRINTJU RKO
020871 RENO NEVADA 12-19 8967A TNT
YRON ICS IPMBGGC
(FONE & ZIP)

1-078945H33 12/19/86
ICS HYPHEA II SS
IISS SM MAD 19 1075

DDD FICTION CITY KO
FICA 666 TOFU 19 ZAP 520 KKK 121
ISBN CO CASH 427
CHICAGO 56/98 19 1515

TF7568365
MR D. WRITER
8431 ARIOLA DRIVE
FICTION CITY KO 76522

    PLYWOOD ANGELS
    ENTER THE CAFETERIA
    SAD MUSIC
    VERMILION TREES
    BLUE MOUNTAINS
    LIKE YESTERDAY

                         BIRD

COL TR Y78654 FICTION CITY YU 876544443
01 912
65-12-14-43-51-23-42-36 19 H

NNN
6092 EAST

1203 EAST

2134 EAST

MGMCOMP MGMFOX BY RKO

TO REPLY BY MAILGRAM MESSAGE, SEE
REVERSE SIDE FOR WESTERN UNION
TOLL-FREE NUMBERS

received a video cassette in the mail. It took me over an hour to locate a VCR and settle down in front of the TV.

Bird was lying in a reclining chair. The back was tilted as far down as it would go and, along with the part on which you rest your legs, it formed an almost horizontal plane. The lighting, extremely muted, made it look as though Bird's body were floating in the black chair. Behind two curtainless windows you could see the dark night and a neon sign blinking on and off. You could also distinguish some noise from the street. A lock of Bird's hair was blowing in the breeze from the open windows. Her body, curved slightly sideways, looked peaceful. She was sleeping in her black T-shirt, her jeans were unzipped. She was wearing blue socks.

At times she would shift her position. A little while later, I saw her eyelids quiver. The fingers of her right hand, resting on her hip, were trembling as well. The camera must have been on a tripod because the angle never shifted. The lighting was rather yellow. I could hear Bird's breathing. Eventually, I discovered the minuscule mike attached to her T-shirt.

Now her body was completely still, in a dreamless sleep. Her parted lips came together with each breath. The lighting accentuated their fullness. This long still shot allowed her to emit a sensuality that was rendered almost unwholesome by the absence of dreams. I imagined Bird's mind completely blank, a lapse into total silence until the next dream sequence began. I wondered about the meaning of this "gift." True, she'd watched me while I was asleep, or at least she'd thought I was, whereas I'd never been accorded the same pleasure. On the other hand, as much as I was enjoying her gift, I could hardly believe that it wasn't a cover-up for some form of cruelty, some kind of vengeance. All of this was too peaceful. She let herself go too much.

Later on, she rolled over slightly, now lying completely on her back, with one hand on her belly and the other almost touching the floor. Judging from the size of the video case, I knew it was a two-hour tape. There was a faint noise coming from off camera, but I was unable to identify it. The more it played on, the more my gaze, encompassing the totality of my senses, reduced the frame of the shot, so that only Bird's body remained.

Her face was turned toward the camera. I was moved by the line of her closed eyelids, her dark, thick eyebrows which nearly met. Her forehead was relaxed, strands of her tangled hair flew out in every direction. Gradually, I became aware of the special quality of the lighting, which sculpted the contours of her body so beautifully. I couldn't decide whether it was due to the artistic talents of the director or simply an accident. I looked at my watch. If the tape were to run without interruption, there were only forty minutes of it left. The thought that there was still more to watch suddenly filled me with joy. Yet I couldn't get rid of a certain anxiety that increased as the time passed. I knew something would occur to destroy the intensity that was binding us together at that moment. Several anticipatory images crossed my mind, but since nothing happened, I gradually calmed down and began to enjoy myself again.

The disproportion of her body, so small on the screen, troubled me. I wondered whether it was possible to rent one of those TVs that projects the picture on a giant screen. I resolved to try and find one the very next day, inasmuch as Bird would possibly be sending me more cassettes. I had several questions about the identity of the filmmaker but it hardly mattered to me. He was offering me a rare privilege. It was also plausible that Bird had set up the camera on a tripod herself, and that she'd also chosen that lighting. Then the only question was why the film began precisely at the moment when she'd fallen asleep. I examined her body and her face with care. They reflected such abandonment that she couldn't have been pretending to be asleep. She gave off a feeling of fluidity. Even the curve of her arm, leaning on the armrest, pulsated with a barely perceptible rhythm. The laughter of two young boys drifted up from the street. I could hear snatches of their conversation, then the silence returned, broken a little while later by a police car's siren.

I was in a state of perfect bliss when suddenly from off camera came a very pure voice. The filmmaker must have put on a tape. From the very first measures, I recognized the aria sung by Cherubino in *The Marriage of Figaro*. I listened with delight to the lyrics:

Non so più cosa son, cosa faccio,
Or di foco, ora sono di ghiaccio,
Ogni donna cangiar di colore,
Ogni donna mi fa palpitar . . .
Ogni donna mi fa palpitar . . .
Ogni donna mi fa palpitar . . .
Solo ai nomi d'amor, di diletto,
Mi si turba, mi s'altera il petto,
E a parlare mi sforza d'amore,
Un desio, un desio ch'io non posso spiegar!
Un desio, un desio ch'io non posso spiegar . . .
Non so più cosa son, cosa faccio,
Or di foco, ora sono di ghiaccio,
Ogni donna cangiar di colore,
Ogni donna mi fa palpitar . . .
Ogni donna mi fa palpitar . . .
Ogni donna mi fa palpitar . . .
Parlo d'amor vegliando,
Parlo d'amor sognando,
All'aqua, all'ombra, ai monti,
Ai fiori, all'erbe, ai fonti,
All'eco, all'aria, ai venti,
Che il suon dei vani accenti,
Portano via con sè . . .
Portano via con sè . . .
Parlo d'amor vegliando,
Parlo d'amor sognando,
All'aqua, all'ombra, ai monti,

Ai fiori, all'erbe, ai fonti,
All'eco, all'aria, ai venti,
Che il suon dei vani accenti,
Portano via con sè . . .
Portano via con sè . . .
E se non ho chi m'oda,
E se non ho chi m'oda,
Parlo d'amor con me, con me,
Parlo d'amor con me.

As soon as the aria was over, the silence returned and it was only several seconds later that my thoughts switched back to Bird's body. I could scarcely believe that this had been her idea. She was completely ignorant about classical music. Of course, she might have heard this melody and have been affected by its beauty, as I was. But if she had chosen this for me to hear, there had to have been a reason.

She had remained in the same position, bestowing on my eyes the gift of her beauty, with the infinite patience of sleep. All of a sudden, I noticed the extreme flatness of her chest. Ordinarily, you could always see her breasts, but they seemed to have disappeared. It was then that I understood why she'd chosen the aria by Cherubino and the double ambiguity it suggested, since the role of the disguised young man (in love with the countess) was sung by a woman. I realized that Bird must have bound her chest to make it appear like that.

I went back to the beginning of the tape and saw that Bird's breasts were nonexistent. The image was utterly androgynous.

In fact, her unzipped jeans, which I'd first interpreted as a simple question of comfort, formed a triangle over her dark hair. This completed the picture.

What was Bird's goal in establishing this deep and subtle bond between us? Was there something more to decipher in this beautiful and mysterious message?

I let the tape play on until the end.

The intensity of the light faded into total darkness. Only the neon sign continued to blink on and off, but it wasn't enough to illuminate Bird's body. I waited, staring at the green neon. Then I heard some background noises, one being the typical sound of a mike brushing against something as it's being removed.

I was tempted to get out of my chair and speed things up by seeing what was ahead, but I didn't budge. My heart was pounding, my hands were clammy. Little by little, the light returned. The reclining chair was empty. The tape was over.

That night, I couldn't sleep, haunted by the androgynous image of Bird, by the music, and by Death, whose presence felt so near that I could hear his breathing.

A letter from Bird written on a scrap of brown paper bag, ripped into a square:

> To see you die. One of these days I'll call you, and we'll fix a meeting place. You'll travel all the way across America and when you arrive, I'll be there and we'll fuck.
>
> Bird

Bird is crossing a desert.

Most of the surface of the moon resembles a monotonous terrain, studded with small craters and littered with rock fragments. The powdery soil is heavily trampled by the two-hour exploration. The landscapes lack color, being variously reported by the astronauts as a uniform dark gray, or sometimes gray with a hint of a warmer tone. But the astronauts were fascinated by the harsh contrasts of light and shadow, unsoftened by an atmosphere. "It has a stark beauty all its own," said Armstrong.

A train ride along the Mississippi. Bird is sitting in the car with panoramic windows, next to the snack bar. The Chameleon is dozing in front of the petrified forests. Whenever his head drops too abruptly he wakes up, opens his eyes wide, takes out the bottle of rum that he keeps in the inside pocket of his jacket, and takes a swig. With a moo moo here and a moo moo there, here a cluck, there a cluck, everywhere a cluck cluck. Shabby little farms. A black woman stretches in the sun, smiling blankly. The Chameleon is getting closer to her. Now she's laughing. The Chameleon discovers that the colors are gradually changing. The river is lemon yellow, the trees turquoise blue, the sky a metallic gray.

The train crosses the suburbs of Chicago. Junkyards stacked with piles of wrecked cars, towering walls of broken dreams. Decrepit brick buildings, trucks and cars abandoned under bridges. The gates of hell.

Tops of skyscrapers jut into the mist. The Chameleon follows Bird. At certain moments, she feels his harsh breathing on the nape of her neck. She turns around, but he's just like the fog, he evaporates and distills.

Bird enters the Hotel Caesar. Sitting on a stool with an unlit cigar dangling between his lips, the obese, crew-cutted proprietor has already anticipated Bird's question:

"Twenty dollars a day, paid in advance. Two-dollar key deposit. No visitors, no phone calls, no drugs."

An old woman walks up to Bird.

"It's less dangerous to sleep in your car than in this hotel."

The Chameleon sees that Bird is hesitating. Right when he's so exhausted. It's bad timing. He's ready to sleep anywhere. Bird pays, takes the key and goes upstairs. The Chameleon flops onto the bed. It's like being in a hammock. Bird takes off her boots, and lies down underneath the covers with all her clothes on. The Chameleon snuggles up next to her. He's finally warming up.

They meet again at the Blackstone Hotel, in the lounge that's been turned into a jazz club. The Chameleon admires the large hallway, the cushioned chairs, the sofas, the woodwork, the spiral staircase, the old elevators. A place where he'd gladly live out his old age—but how could he contemplate relaxation when here he was, running from one corner of the country to the other, trying not to lose track of two completely erratic characters?

The Chameleon lets Bird go into the club, takes advantage of the situation and steals a hamburger from a customer who's busy looking for his credit cards.

A curved bar. The decor is from the thirties. Pillars. Lilac walls, pearl-gray ceilings. Sunk down in an armchair, Bird is looking at the giant photo of Charlie Parker. Young. Handsome. Smiling. Well dressed. His sax, jumping right out of the picture.

McCoy Tyner is playing "Round Midnight."

At three in the morning, they change hotels. They take a room at the Blackstone.

She's having a dream, her lips are moving. The Chameleon leans over Bird's face. He inhales her breath.

Sunset Strip. The tall palm trees bend in the wind. Bird is wearing a new cone-shaped hat with a tassel, made of peach-colored Chinese silk. She passes a school just as the children are being let out, then in front of the motels to the left and right of the Strip.

She chooses one called the Starlight, with a fixed price of twenty-two dollars. She climbs a few steps and walks over to the office window. A Vietnamese woman comes out.

Bird: "I'd like a room."

The Vietnamese woman: "Twenty-six dollars."

Bird: "It says twenty-two on the sign outside."

The Vietnamese woman: "We can't keep changing the sign every year."

Bird pays and is given her key.

The Vietnamese woman: "The left stairway."

The balconies have protective bars around them. You can't get out without passing by the office. Bird reaches her room. A worn and greasy green carpet. Holes in the sheets and a night table covered with cigarette burns. The television is attached to the wall with a swinging metal bar. The closet has no door, no hangers. Bird throws her bag on the bed. She switches the light on in the bathroom. The bugs disappear down the drainpipes of the bathtub and sink.

Bird lies down on the bed and gazes at the pine and eucalyptus trees through the open door.

From the next room, Bird recognizes "Round Midnight" by Thelonious Monk, being played in roughly twelve different versions, one right after the other. She listens, lets herself ease into the music. She gradually reaches a kind of ecstasy, reflected in her expression and her body.

Bird slips some coins into the soda machine. She opens the can of Coke and heads back toward her room. As she gets nearer, the "Round Midnight" theme returns. She stops in front of the door next to hers, listens for a moment, then decides to knock.

Corlina: "Come in . . ."

Bird pushes the door open. Corlina, a massive black sculpture of a woman with ebony curves, looks more like a goddess than a human being. Her enormous mouth breaks into a smile. Without moving from the bed, where she's lying as if on a pedestal, she starts to laugh.

Bird: "Do you want some Coke?"

Corlina: "Come over and sit down."

Bird makes herself comfortable on the bed. She holds out the can to Corlina, who barely lifts her head to take a sip.

Bird: "It's one of my favorite tunes."

Corlina: "Did you just get here?"

Bird: "A few hours ago, on the bus."

Corlina: "Is this your first time in L.A.?"

Bird: "Yes."

Corlina: "What are you going to do here?"

Bird: "Nothing in particular. Take a long walk. What about you?"

Corlina: "I sleep. I listen to 'Round Midnight.' I've spent so many nights hanging around on street corners, ever since I was twelve. I've got to catch up on a lot of sleep. I've been here for five weeks now. I've had a few customers that the other girls sent over, but right now I'm pretty hard up and I'm hungry."

Corlina opens the drawer of the night table. There are two ten-dollar bills and some change.

Corlina: "Take this and go buy two roast chickens. There's a store across the street, in the shopping center."

In the nearby supermarket, Bird buys two chickens, some French fries, and some apples, mangoes, some bread and a bottle of wine. She also buys some indigo-blue mascara and an eye pencil in the same color.

Corlina is sitting on the bed. She's gotten out of the shower. The water is still dripping down her shoulders and arms. She's dried herself with a towel that's now wrapped around her torso. Bird takes the groceries out of the bag, and uncorks the wine.

Bird: "I brought you some mascara and an eye pencil."

Corlina: "How did you know that was my favorite color?"

Bird: " 'Mood Indigo.' "

They laugh and devour the food. Corlina attacks the chicken, tears it apart with her strong hands, and gulps it down in huge mouthfuls.

Bird: "You eat the bones?"

Corlina: "It's good for your teeth."

Bird: "You have incredibly powerful jaws."

Corlina: "One day, I ate the wallet of a guy who didn't want to pay, with everything in it: driver's license, Social Security card, money, pictures of his wife and his dog. Luckily, it was good leather."

Corlina crunches on the bones, drinks a half pint at each sip, bites a chunk of an apple, while Bird sits there, fascinated.

Bird: "You're very beautiful."

Corlina: "If I could only stay awake and go cruise the streets once in a while, I'd be able to open my own bank. I sleep at least twenty hours a day."

Bird: "Like wild cats do."

Corlina: "They do that?"

Bird: "They sleep, they hunt, they eat, they fuck, and climb back up in the trees for a snooze."

Corlina: "I'd love to do that, sleep in a tree. I'm from Atlanta. I have a little girl who's twelve and a little boy who's eight. When I was fifteen, I started working for a guitar player I was crazy about. He needed money for his habit. Later on I dumped him but kept on working a little here, a little there. One day, I realized that if I could sleep while my clients were screwing me, it would be much nicer than becoming a junkie or an alcoholic. By sheer concentration, it started to work. In the beginning, just little lapses, then gradually, I could fall asleep as soon as I was lying down. The only problem was, I got ripped off a lot when it came time to pay."

Bird: "I can help you."

Corlina: "If you walk up the Strip, you'll see the Actor's Guild on the right. There are three or four girls who work that corner. Ask for Cyd. She's a friend of mine. She'll let you recruit a customer for me."

Bird walks slowly up the street, looking at every car. A man slows down, stops and opens his window.

The customer: "How much?"

Bird: "Fifty."

The customer: "In this neighborhood, you don't have to bend over backward to pick up girls who do it for thirty."

Bird turns around and walks away. The customer catches up with her. His face is illuminated for an instant as he lights a cigarette.

The customer: "Let's go."

Bird: "Go park your car. It's right nearby."

Bird and the customer walk into Corlina's room. She's asleep, naked, and has painted her lids and eyelashes indigo blue. The customer looks at her.

The customer: "She's high as a kite on junk . . ."

Bird: "No, she's asleep."

The customer: "Is she the one I'm supposed to . . ."

Bird: "Lay out your money."

The customer counts the bills and holds them out to her.

The customer: "Strange, this thing of yours. Is she going to sleep the whole time?"

Bird: "In ten minutes, you're out of here."

The customer gets undressed. Bird watches the TV. The bed creaks. She glances distractedly at Corlina, then eats a banana.

Just as Bird finishes her banana, the man holds back a groan. He gets up and puts his clothes back on.

The customer: "Not bad, this thing of yours, it's a little like fucking a corpse. Anyway, it's no different with any of you, that's the way it always is."

Bird stands up, and the man walks out the door.

Corlina: "Bird . . . Bird . . ."

She's in Corlina's arms, burying herself in the dark massive body, bathed in the silver reflection of the afternoon light. Bird is curled up in a fetal position. Corlina caresses her until she emerges from her deep sleep.

There are several hundred dollars on the night table.

Corlina: "How long have we been together?"

Bird: "Three . . ."

Corlina: "Every time I wake up, you're asleep. I went into your room and brought over your things."

Bird: "I wish I could stay here, next to you, forever. You smell good. I feel like I'm in a kind of never-ending dream."

Corlina: "No one's keeping you from staying."

Bird: "Did you see the money?"

Corlina: "What did the guys say?"

Bird: "I was watching TV. You really don't feel anything?"

Corlina: "The motel could go up in smoke before I'd notice."

Bird: "I'm going to buy some doughnuts and coffee."

Corlina and Bird have breakfast in bed as they listen to "Round Midnight." Corlina is naked, Bird is fully dressed. She's wearing her hat.

Corlina: "The other day on TV, I saw a movie about Monk. He was magnificent. Something magic was coming out of that piano. He was wearing a hat like yours. The music was so beautiful that he already looked half dead, like a statue, a mummy. As though it were just his spirit flowing through his old fingers."

Bird: "I had a picture of him in my bag. One of Charlie Parker too."

Corlina: "Sometimes I think about my children. They're so far away! We could keep on working, buy a car, and travel across country. A car, or a camper that we could sleep in."

Bird: "I could drive . . ."

Corlina: "I've dreamed about so many things in my life . . ."

It's nighttime. Bird and Corlina are in each other's arms, asleep. You can hear the song of a cardinal in the eucalyptus tree outside.

Later. Corlina is lying on her back, arms and legs spread wide apart, taking up the entire bed. Bird is stretched out on the floor, lying on a blanket.

It's daybreak. Bird wakes up, goes into the bathroom, pees, and comes back.

Corlina is still in the same position. Her lips are moving and she's murmuring something. Bird moves closer to try to understand what she's saying, but Corlina is speaking some obscure language that sounds like an African dialect. Bird caresses Corlina's body, kisses her, soothes her. When all is quiet again, Bird climbs onto the bed and curls up between Corlina's formidable legs, which coil tightly around her. Bird's head is resting on the ebony woman's mound, like a newborn child. Lulled by the peaceful rhythm of her breathing, Bird falls asleep with her hands on Corlina's breasts.

Bird awakens in the light-flooded room. Her hand gropes for Corlina. Bird gets up with a start and glances around. Corlina's things are gone. All that remains is the cassette player, a few tapes, and half the money. Bird finds a note on her bed, which she reads. Tears. She's racked with increasingly violent spasms, she sobs, she screams, she buries her head in the pillow, she curls up in a ball, then, suddenly, her body unfolds, she tears at the sheets, the pillows, bolts out of bed, rips the television from the wall, throws it out the window, grabs hold of the night table, smashes it against the bed and destroys the room before collapsing in the midst of the debris.

Finally, the promised rendezvous. After days of wandering, fatigue, and surprises, I found a series of messages left by Bird. One in a phone booth. Another in a hotel room. Another in a gas station. Hadn't we been playing games long enough? Was this an end, a beginning, or simply a stinging reminder?

The road climbed upward. At every turn, as far as the eyes could see, a panoramic view of the mountains, irrevocably green. I'd lose one radio station only to find another. After the incessant movement of the ocean, the forest seemed monochromatic, devoid of any charm. Somewhere in the process of waiting so long and searching from place to place for Bird, my longing for her had started to wane. But in the morning, in the cold hotel rooms where thousands had left their scent of solitude, I'd be seized by a rough desire and the images would flicker through my mind until the road finally reentered my consciousness.

I was amazed that Bird hadn't chosen a stranger place than this. I turned off the main highway, onto a dirt road that led to a lake. I got out and walked until I came to a log cabin. I realized I was there alone, that the cabin was empty, that this was the end of our game of hide-and-seek. I'd hoped for the city, the swarming masses, the raw nerves; I found a decaying carcass swinging from a beam.

.   .   .

Looking out the bay window of her room, Bird gazes at the runway, the green and blue lights, the planes that are taking off and landing almost silently. Naked in the darkness, she presses her body against the cold pane of glass and in her husky voice recites a poem by Coleridge, written down in one of his notebooks.

> "Smile in the eye
> An Incarnation of the Soul in Light—
> A light, a living Light, that is at once
> Language, & Thought, & Feeling—"

ithout knowing why, Bird opens up a sixteenth-century French dictionary to the page where "Albino" is listed, and finds this definition: "White Negro who sees best at night."

She closes the book, gets up, crosses the vast reading room and, suddenly, she spots him, in the light of the green lamp, also hunched over a book. He's wearing a crocheted wool hat with a black and white pattern. She recognizes his profile. She's positive that it's him. His face is so close to the page that she can't make out his features. Or at least the line of his nose. It's him, it's the Chameleon. If she moves closer, will he evaporate into thin air once again? Will he turn into a book?

She moves away, never taking her eyes off him, hides behind a pillar and waits.

The Chameleon gets up. He abandons his reading. Bird approaches and takes his seat. The book looks brand new, as if it had never been opened. Printed in silver letters on the black cloth is the title: CANNIBAL KISS.

Bird rushes toward the stairway where the Chameleon has just disappeared. She runs down the stairs, hesitates a moment in front of the door to the men's room, then decides to go in.

She thinks she sees an image in one of the mirrors. A blurry gray shape on the run. A face that seems incapable of any expression other than suffering. But as soon as she tries to move closer, she's alone again, she hears the water flushing in the urinals, then nothing at all.

Fires. A deserted street in the Bronx. Caved-in buildings, burned-out cars, piles of garbage. It's getting dark. Bird is twirling a piece of plastic tubing in a circle over her head that gives off a low sound, which varies in pitch according to the speed of rotation.

A few shadowy figures come out of the dilapidated buildings. A little black girl with straightened braids moves up closer.

"Who brought you here?"

"The police."

"Why?"

"I fell out of the sky."

"Why are you naked?"

"I'm not an astronaut. When I travel in the sky, I prefer to be naked."

"Why is your body painted blue?"

"I *am* blue, I am the darkness, I am the shadows. Blue is the color that links day with night."

"What do you mean by that?"

"Exactly what you heard."

"Where are you right now?"

"Sitting across from a psychiatrist."

"What day is it today?"

"Tuesday or Wednesday."

"What year?"

"When it comes to the universe, no one can really be sure."

"Who's our President right now?"

"That all depends on which society you're referring to."

"Are you employed?"

"Jumping is part of my job."

"Could you clarify that statement?"

"I had a one-year contract with a writer, it's my last day of work."

"What is your level of education?"

"I finished my master's degree in literature and I started working for him. For the ending, I painted my body the color blue you have right in front of you. I hijacked a small tourist plane, I stole a parachute and I jumped."

"Would you care to specify the nature of the contract between you and this writer."

"Oral."

"You mean to say that you didn't sign anything?"

"You might say that."

"Were you paid?"

"He sent me half of his salary."

"What did you give him in return?"

"Material."

"What kind of material?"

"Life material."

"Can you give me his name, his address and phone number?"

"No."

"Have you ever consulted anyone outside the medical profession?"

"No."

"Are you a member of a religious community, or a sect that prohibits the consultation of a doctor?"

"No."

"Are you in good health?"

"I guess so."

"Does your body function normally?"

"It works."

"Have you ever been subject to anxiety during these last few months?"

"I kept wondering where the wind would carry me to land."

"Then you didn't intend to land in the parking lot of a shopping center?"

"No, I'd planned it to be on the beach."

"Was this the first time you ever jumped?"

"Yes."

"When you're worried, do your thoughts spin inside your head?"

"I was falling too fast for that to happen."

"When you're preoccupied, can you change your train of thought and turn your mind to another subject?"

"Sometimes."

"Do you ever get headaches? Do you have the feeling your head is in a vise, that your scalp is tight, pains at the nape of your neck?"

"No."

"Do you ever feel a fatigue that's not caused by work or exercise?"

"No."

"Do you experience muscular tension, do you have trouble relaxing?"

"No."

"Are you excitable, do you pace back and forth in a room without taking the time to sit down?"

"Sometimes."

"Do you worry about your health?"

"No. I always think about the fact that I'm going to die, but I don't really worry about it. It's just a habit."

"Do you sometimes have the impression you're on the verge of a nervous breakdown?"

"Only when I go for a few days without sleep."

"Do you do that often?"

"When I'm working."

"Give me some examples."

"I spent a whole week in a movie theater, another in a bar."

"That was part of your job?"

"Yes."

"Does noise disturb you?"

"I like noise."

"Do you have the feeling that the noise can penetrate right into your head?"

"Into my head, my body, that's what I like."

"Do you have trouble breathing?"

"Sometimes at night I feel like I can't breathe or swallow my saliva."

"Is your mouth usually dry?"

"No, only when I drink."

"Do you perspire a lot?"

"When I have a good fuck, yes."

"Do you have palpitations, shaking spells?"

"No."

"Do you ever have the feeling that you're floating?"

"I float a lot."

"What makes you feel like you're floating?"

"Music, traveling through space."

"Do you ever have the feeling that something terrible might happen?"

"That's usually when it happens, isn't it?"

"Are you afraid to get up in the morning, to face a new day?"

"If that's the case, I stay in bed."

"Have you ever had feelings of panic in everyday situations, like while you're taking the bus, walking into a room, or making a phone call?"

"No, only when someone tried to kill me."

"Could you tell me more about that?"

"No, it was part of my job."

"Do you think that the job you were asked to do was a normal one?"

"We're talking about a writer."

"Have you ever felt anxiety in a crowd, in closed spaces, like tunnels, elevators, phone booths?"

"Yes, in a phone booth. I once stayed there five days. A long conversation."

"For your job?"

"Out of curiosity."

"And in open spaces?"

"In the sky."

"Have you ever had trouble eating, drinking or writing in front of other people?"

"Yeah, one time at breakfast in a coffee shop. This disgusting guy sitting across from me took off his shirt and started scratching himself."

"Are you afraid of heights, hurricanes, the dark, blood, open wounds, animals or insects?"

"Hurricanes. When I was a few months old, a tornado destroyed our house and carried me two miles away, to a cornfield."

"Are you under the impression that you're able to think clearly, without any outside interference?"

"I like interferences."

"Are you able to concentrate easily?"

"Yes."

"Have you been neglecting yourself?"

"If I were, I wouldn't have painted myself blue."

"Have you taken an interest in new things recently?"

"That's all I've done for the past year."

"Does your memory sometimes go blank?"

"I've never heard of a memory that doesn't. The blanks are what allow us to survive."

"Do you control your own thoughts?"

"I'm not under that kind of illusion."

"Do you have the feeling that some people can read your mind?"

"I'm not exactly an open book, not yet, anyway."

"Have you cried recently?"

"Yes."

"What was your last pleasant experience?"

"When I jumped."

"How do you see the future?"

"I live from day to day."

"Do you think that life is worth living?"

"The way I live it, yes."

"Suicidal thoughts?"

"No, I just kept hoping the damned parachute would open."

"Do you eat regularly?"

"More than regularly."

"Have you had trouble sleeping?"

"I don't sleep much, but when I do, it's great."

"Do some things seem to happen too fast?"

"Not fast enough."

"Have you experienced a loss of sexual appetite?"

"On the contrary."

"Do you often get angry?"

"I get violent."

"How does that manifest itself?"

"I try not to kill people."

"Have you ever experienced the feeling of power?"

"It wasn't just a feeling."

"Are you sometimes overwhelmed by thoughts or exciting ideas?"

"I've gotten used to having my ideas and my desires realized to an impossible extent."

"Do you think you have any extraordinary talents, a great potential?"

"Obviously."

"Do you feel that you must verify certain things that you've just done?"

"No."

"Do you spend a lot of time washing, even when there's no need?"

"I've nothing against a little dirt."

"Are you aware of performing any body rituals?"

"Is pissing a ritual?"

"Do you constantly ask yourself questions about the meaning of the universe?"

"The meaning of the universe . . . Are you really thinking about what you're saying?"

"Do you have the feeling that everything around you is unreal?"

"Constantly."

"How does that feel?"

"Reassuring."

"Have you ever felt like you were unreal?"

"I am unreal, I'm a character in a novel."

"Has it ever happened that you were unable to see your own reflection in the mirror?"

"No."

"Have you ever had the feeling that certain parts of your body don't belong to you anymore?"

"I'd call that an orgasm."

"Does your imagination play tricks on you?"

"It doesn't play, it works."

"Have you ever noticed anything unusual in terms of shapes, sounds, odors, taste or the consistency of certain things?"

"If you go into a bar and decide to suck on everything you find, you'd be pretty surprised about the way things taste."

"Did you ever do that?"

"I told you, I'm curious."

"Do objects sometimes look distorted to you?"

"When I get violent, objects tend to change shape but it's not an illusion."

"Do you think you appear normal to others?"

"Being normal doesn't interest me."

"Do you think that your perception of time ever changes?"

"Constantly."

"Do you think that you've lost your emotional capacities?"

"They're unlimited."

"Have you ever had hallucinations?"

"Fortunately."

"What kind?"

"All kinds."

"Were you awake?"

"Yes."

"How do you explain it?"

"I've never been particularly fascinated by explanations."

"Is there someone who controls your actions?"

"I'm uncontrollable."

"Why?"

"I'm fast, unpredictable. Even 'he' couldn't do it."

"Have you ever been subject to amnesia, or a loss of bodily sensations?"

"No."

"Do you take drugs or medicine?"

"I've taken drugs: Ecstasy, cocaine, but very little for the past year."

"Why?"

"To be under the illusion of reality."

"Have you ever perceived unusual colors in your environment?"

"Sky blue isn't blue when you're traveling through it."

"How much alcohol do you drink?"

"Not much. Sometimes none at all."

"Do you think you have a problem?"

"I had a problem landing. That's about it."

In a room lit by moonlight, Bird, her sleep disturbed by the restless dreams of the Chameleon, keeps changing positions. The Chameleon is getting off a train. The concourse of the train station, a huge baroque building painted pink, is overrun with a multicolored crowd of people who are waiting. The Chameleon feels like he's being watched, observed. They're approaching him, they're touching him, they're speaking to him in strange tongues. A young boy even goes so far as to tickle him with an ear of wheat.

The lunar mountains, a region of peaks that is abundantly covered with craters, are older than the lunar seas. They must have originally resembled the soil of the moon at the time of its formation: a no-man's-land of various blocks and exploded craters; they were never subjected to fusion—hence, never levelled—since the beginning of the solar system. These mountains, whose exploration was the purpose of the *Apollo 15* and *16* expeditions, were not viewed by the first *Apollo* landings because they were situated on very risky terrain. Photographs taken of the "coastline" of the Ocean of Tempests provide evidence that supports the theory that the mountains are the older formation. The smooth surface of the Ocean of Tempests adjacent to the mountains seemed to fill a basin in the rocky terrain which formed these mountains. It is likely that the mountains existed first, and that the basin was hollowed out later by the fall of a giant meteorite. Subsequently, the lava accumulated in the basin, exactly like the waters on the earth accumulate in the natural basins of the earth's crust. This conclusion is reinforced by the fact that the thickness of the craters on the mountains is greater than those on the seas, indicating that they were bombarded by meteorites for a longer time.

ird had slipped on one of my shirts. She rolled up the blue cotton sleeves. The shirttails came down to her thighs. She was sitting on the wooden deck, her feet in the sand, drinking tea. The wind was blowing the shirt flat against her body and sweeping back her dark hair. The ocean was rough this morning, and an ashen fog joined the horizon with the sky. The seagulls had retreated inland. The beach was deserted.

She didn't hear me coming. I sat down next to her. She was looking at the ocean. I poured myself a cup of lukewarm tea.

"I can hardly believe that you've lived in this house for a whole year now. There's something inhuman about this beauty. You have to be crazy to be able to stand it. I got up just before the sun. I walked a few miles with my feet in the water. The beach was covered with frozen jellyfish. I touched them. They're smooth and icy. A little like your brain. The further I walked, the more I had the feeling that each jellyfish was carrying a chapter of your book inside it. At one point I stopped, I stretched out in the sand and I put a jellyfish on my stomach until it got soft and slimy. It was beautiful out at six o'clock. I took a swim and then dried off in the wind. Do you want to lick me? I'm full of salt."

Bird lifted the shirt above her breasts with one hand, and

pulled me toward her with the other. I placed my lips on her left breast, one hand balancing on the deck and the other on her hip. My tongue got a taste of Bird permeated by the ocean.

"That's exactly the kind of breakfast you need."

I went to make some fresh tea and returned to the deck with a few slices of toast and a chunk of Cheddar.

"I saw some black fish. They were diamond-shaped, there were four of them. They were playing near the shore."

"Those were flounders. A few weeks ago, I went swimming with some dolphins. They stayed right next to me for more than an hour. They kept rubbing up against me."

"If everyone did exactly what he wanted, just by following his instinct from one moment to the next, what do you think would happen?"

Bird took a few sips of tea.

"Are you going back to the university?"

"No. I'll send my manuscript to some publishers and then I'll wait."

"And if nobody publishes it?"

"I don't know."

"There are too many big chunks of my life in this book. And they're the ones that you invented from what I gave you. Now I have an urge to take those things back. It's my turn to suck the marrow out of your bones."

"Why did you have me come all the way across the country, just to suck the marrow out of my bones, as you put it? Why didn't you do the same to me? What were you afraid of?"

"Of destroying you. Of destroying your book."

"Maybe that's why I'm here."

"The last time we saw each other, when I was leaving for a year, I thought you'd make me dissolve, that you'd reabsorb me. I had moments of fear. Sheer terror. The more I moved forward, the more I accentuated your desire, and the more I felt an embryo forming inside me. And the further I went, the more I could sense that my fear and anxiety were diminishing."

"Did you write anything, besides what you sent me?"

"I tried. I know why all those fragments of yours that I read have remained fragments. In the beginning, I kept a journal which I later destroyed. The simple act of relating what I was experiencing required so much energy that I didn't have any left to live my life. Reading through what I'd written during the first six weeks, I realized that everything was heading toward degradation, toward a decline. It's a vicious circle. Afterwards, when I got rid of it, I felt suddenly liberated."

"Why is sex such a priority with you?"

"That's a part of who I am. When I fuck someone, I expose him, I strip off his varnish, I turn him inside out, I photograph his soul, I make his cells explode, I send him off in space, I intoxicate him, I feed him, I push his life right to the edge of the cliff. I enjoy seeing his face at that very moment, during those few seconds when he has nothing left to hold on to, when he's completely naked. That's what gives me pleasure, that's what sends me skyrocketing into space. It's the most powerful sensation I know. It's the only one that exceeds the limit of the greatest possible pleasure combined with the worst possible pain. And the people who I fuck with know all about this feeling. It has nothing to do with love. It's stronger, it's right then and there, and it leaves no bitter aftertaste. There's no regret. There's nothing else like it. I loved Corlina, I loved the Albino, Boto, and all the others. I gave them my tenderness and my fragility. They lived inside me. Everyone else ceases to exist, they fade into white, then they're annihilated, pulverized. The only trace they leave behind looks something like the tail of a comet."

"What's left for them?"

"The same thing. An abstract glimmer. A body slashed to pieces. They have no more fantasies, no illusions left. They expect nothing more. First I absorbed them, nourished them, then at the most intense moment, I gave birth to them. Now, they're somewhere else, in another dimension."

Bird stood up to take a walk along the beach.

The writer searches the beach. The white sand stretches as far as the eye can see. Not a trace of her. Bird has disappeared.

A white cat is mewing. The waves, fairly rough this morning, are breaking in an ever-changing rhythm. A Navy helicopter flies over the beach. The propeller generates dry throbbing gusts of air that soon merge with the breaking waves.

The air, charged with iodine, mixes with the resinous odor of the wooden planks from the deck, heated by the sun.

The writer plucks a tiny succulent plant out of the sand, growing among the tall weeds. He fingers the leaves, which are smooth, thick, hard.

The writer finishes his cold and bitter tea, full of tannin.

As the days go by, whenever he leaves the house the feeling of moving into another kind of space becomes increasingly subtle. The inside is for work, creation, and sleep. It's through the power of his mind that he can make it expand, transforming it until it no longer exists. The outdoors provides him with a space that can be adapted to his daily moods, to the success or failure of his work, to the dimension created through his contact with words. There's always some kind of musical concordance between the two spaces, and his body either revels in it or suffers from the intense power of these harmonies or dissonances.

This morning, the writer has the sense of an open space which seems almost unlimited. It's as if his skin no longer exists, as if it had suddenly dissolved, then evaporated.

During this past year, his body had changed. He'd become aware of muscles he'd never really used before. It had been a kind of slow process of building himself up through walking, breathing, stillness, the contact with the water, the receding tide of trivial thoughts. He had delighted in this mechanical sensation. His every movement was stimulated by countless chain reactions.

There's a cool breeze in spite of the sun. The writer goes back inside and slips on an old sweatshirt.

He closes the sliding glass door and walks down to the beach. His bare feet sink into the sand. Thousands of grains roll under the soles of his feet.

Still five or six more hours until sunset.

Is there any way to determine how far away Bird is? She's beyond his field of vision, at any rate.

. . .

He relaxes his abdominal muscles and takes a deep breath.

He decides to try and catch up with Bird. He imagines the moment when he will see her silhouette in the distance.

The writer has been walking along the beach for more than three hours and Bird hasn't turned up yet. Now the landscape is desertlike; tiny plants sprout in the hollows of dunes of various lunar shapes, which have endlessly shifted ever since he's lived on this beach. He'd quickly learned to appreciate this unrecognizable landscape. Many times before, he would walk until he was completely exhausted and then, during the days that followed, reap the fruits of his labor. Drained of their color, the jellyfish had begun to harden on the sand, ripped apart by the beaks of seagulls and little sandpipers, which flee at his approaching step, then turn around and go back to where they were originally, following the flow of the advancing and ebbing tide, feeding themselves with quick pecking movements, leaving a trail in the sand that vanishes with the next wave.

The wind. The cries of seagulls. A wave breaks at his feet. He's following Bird's footprints. At times they disappear completely, then reappear a little further on. She's been walking right at the water's edge, just as he is.

. . .

He bends down, scoops up a handful of kelp, sniffing it before he throws it back into the ocean.

He likes the feel of this smooth, sticky, pliable substance.

The smell alone makes him feel as if he'd been chewing it, feeding on it.

In this fatigued state, his body lets go of its last barriers, its final formal illusions, even the idea of being in possession of his arms and his legs. Little by little, this feeling creeps into his torso, his pelvis and his head so strongly that the writer no longer has any sense of moving forward or that his body belongs to him.

The final minutes of sun leave a pleasant feeling of warmth on his back and the nape of his neck.

He avoids the waves of the rising tide as much as possible, but tries not to walk in the dry sand, into which his feet sink so heavily that it tires him even more.

The sun disappears, the sky darkens, the dunes lose their contrast.

. . .

He knows that the beach goes on for ever and ever. He has never walked all the way to the end of this narrow strip of sand which runs along the coast. Bird's footprints are lost to infinity.

He's out of breath, intoxicated by the ocean air. He stops, sits down in the sand and gazes at the line of the horizon, jagged with dark ridges.

Maybe Bird has cut through the dunes and decided to walk home by way of the other beach, which is more sheltered from the wind and faces the mainland?

Then the writer notices the imprint of Bird's body. She'd stretched out with her face to the ground and had dug her hands into the sand when she'd stood up. That way, she hadn't spoiled the picture of her body. A half moon had risen. Now the foam is phosphorescent. The dunes are taking on abstract forms.

He hears the delicate song of a bird that seems to be flying overhead. It's the airy two-tone song of a tropical bird.

He breathes, without noticing sea air. His feet have grown numb. His sense of space, which has expanded with the stars, is now gone. His muscles are slack. The air is infiltrating into every fiber. The writer is like one of those bundles of straw that have been washed up by the ocean and tumbled along by the wind in oblong heaps.

Cold.

Loss of verticality. He can walk, though.

A gentle sensation of passing time, bringing sparks of light to his body from near and far away.

The harsh whiteness of the beach is fading into the darkness of the merging sea and sky. There is no longer either exterior or interior.

Where is she?

Naked. Black and white like a photograph. Standing on top of the dune. The writer takes off his clothes. He climbs toward her.

Her dark lips are moving, she's speaking so softly that he's not certain that he's really heard her.

"I'm going to eat you."

She lays him down on the sand and stretches out on top of him. He inhales that scent which has never left him, Bird's scent. It's like walking into a pine forest. Nothing else exists. He touches her in all her warmth. He tastes her body, licking and kissing it. She nibbles. She sucks. They consume each other. Lost in the moonlight, they swallow mouthfuls of sand. The writer can feel her nails digging into him, her teeth lovingly pressed against his skin, making the blood surge. Now he's beginning to experience definite sensations. Her teeth are curved and delicate until they suddenly turn sharp.

When the writer feels Bird's teeth sinking into him deeper and deeper, he does not cry out. He thinks of the word "memory." He remembers, and he also senses something more resilient than skin, something that's inside him, in his mouth, that will soon break away from Bird's body like a morsel of his own flesh. Music.

The helicopter is approaching. A spotlight shines a circle of blue and white at the foot of the dune, where their bodies have rolled. The writer and Bird are pressed close together. The helicopter is hovering in the sky, and the pulsating air from the propeller makes it look as if it were fixed on to a solid backdrop.

The orange gleam of the control panel scarcely illuminates the Chameleon's face or rather the vestiges of a face, the vague impression of a presence observing two bodies in the sand. And behind those vestiges of a face, the sensory organs, a mind, an artist perhaps? It's also possible that the beach is deserted, as it is every morning, that Bird and the writer are a dream, made up by the observer with the blurry face who surfaces every now and then in this story and has finally decided that he's seen enough.

So the helicopter moves off into the distance, the sphere of light spreads into the zone of silence.

DANIEL ODIER was born in 1945. He studied painting in Rome and has taught comparative literature and creative writing at several American universities. Under his own name he has published *The Job,* which was based on his conversations with William Burroughs, and eight novels. He has also published six novels under the name of Delacorta, including *Diva,* on which the international hit film was based.